Horses in the

Jane Ayres

Horses in the Gallery

Illustrated by
Richard Allen

ARMADA

First published in the U.K. in 1990 in Armada

Armada is an imprint of the Children's Division,
part of the Collins Publishing Group,
8 Grafton Street, London W1X 3LA

Copyright © Jane Ayres 1990

Printed and bound in Great Britain by
William Collins Sons & Co. Ltd, Glasgow

CONTENTS

'Shall we go in then?' asked Mo, reading the sign.

'Why not?' replied her twin brother Mark. 'Anyway, it could be our birthday treat.'

Through the door was the first of a series of rooms, all small and dimly lit, with black painted walls. Mo and Mark seemed to be the only people there: not even an attendant stood by to keep an eye on the exhibits.

'It's almost a bit creepy,' said Mark in a low voice.

'But fun,' added Mo.

'The exhibition could be just for us,' said Mark, peering at the first hologram, 'because the first picture is a horse.'

Mo looked over his shoulder. Before them was a magnificent black stallion, his head held proud and high, standing by a river in a forest.

'It looks so real,' gasped Mo. 'The horse looks as though he's moving.'

'That's probably the effect of the hologram,' replied Mark, trying to sound knowledgeable. 'Look, there's a girl standing in the background. Funny, but I didn't notice her before. She's dressed in very old fashioned clothes. I wonder who she is.'

As the twins gazed at the hologram they became aware of more and more detail. It was almost as though it was coming to life before their eyes . . .

Black

The sun glistened on the winding river as Maud followed its passage through the forest. Yellowing leaves squelched underfoot, still sodden from the previous night's heavy rain, brushing the hem of her long linen skirt.

The year was 1349. Maud was in her fifteenth year, a lively young woman of robust constitution. Helping her father and two brothers on their small farm kept her fit and since her mother's death they had come to rely on her as their little mother. But for the next hour she was escaping from the daily household chores to enjoy a walk, pausing only to pick giant mushrooms and blackberries so that her journey would not be considered entirely frivolous.

As she breathed in the damp, musty air she noticed a fellow traveller up ahead. Her eyes hardened as she recognized the familiar black and white garb of the Cistercian monk. Rents and taxes imposed by the monastery on whose land they lived were an extra burden to their already hard lives. Her resentment was increased by her knowledge that the monks had used legal trickery to procure the land.

She watched as the monk stopped by the riverbank and knelt down to take a drink. The recent heavy rainfall had caused the river to rise and Maud wondered if she should warn him to take care. But she held her tongue, telling herself that he would have the sense to realize this. As she bent to pick a particularly attractive looking mushroom, a scream caused her to straighten up. The sticky mud at the river's edge had given way under the monk's weight and he had fallen into the deep murky water. The man's arms flailed and splashed as he struggled to keep afloat. For a second, Maud watched. The monk could not swim.

He had gone under the water twice before Maud decided to act. She did not hate the monk enough to see him drown and quickly she tore off her rough coat and dived into the muddy depths. It was a treacherous river, fast flowing and choked with tough reeds, ready to ensnare the unwary swimmer. But Maud, a strong swimmer, was soon at the side of the startled monk. Luckily he was too tired to struggle or he could have pulled the girl under with him. As it was, Maud was able to drag him to the safety of the bank where they both lay, soaked and exhausted.

'I owe you my life.' The monk regarded her with gratitude. 'I live not far from this place. Let us return and dry our clothes.'

The monastery was humming with activity and Maud felt uneasy within its walls and Gothic arches. The occupants looked up from their work in the gardens to inspect the visitor. She hoped not to encounter the infamous Abbot, whose power she feared.

When she left an hour later, warmed with broth, it was not a moment too soon for her. But on her way to the gate the monk said, 'Wait. I have a gift to repay you.'

Maud turned in surprise as the monk gestured towards the yard. Tethered to an iron ring in the wall was a black horse.

Maud had never seen such a horse. He was blacker than the blackest night, blacker than the devil himself. His noble head was mounted on a strong crested neck, his short back linked to broad quarters. His luxuriant black tail was set low and his mane was long and silky. The horse turned his dished face to look at her, the eyes large and dark, the ears small and alert.

Maud was awed by the beast's enormous presence.

'Such a horse you will not find again. His sire was an Arab and his dam was of the Spanish breed. The king himself would be proud of such a mount.'

'How can I accept such a generous gift?' Maud could not conceal her astonishment.

'You must, if you do not wish to offend. You cannot refuse.' He handed Maud the halter rope.

As she walked home with her prize Maud could not believe her good fortune. The horse was truly a splendid beast and would make a good workhorse, of which the farm was sorely in need. Their own farm horse Geoffrey, was getting old and would need to be replaced in due course.

'Father, look what I have brought!' she called.

Her father emerged from the house, their two dogs close at his heels. But the smile froze on his face when he saw the horse.

'Take that beast away before it is too late,' he said in a voice that chilled her to the bone.

'But, father, what is wrong? What have I done?'

'The horse is cursed.'

'How can that be? He was given, as a reward.'

'Whose gift?'

'One of the monks'. I rescued him from drowning.'

Her father spat at the ground and the horse jumped back in alarm. 'Some reward. They mean to drive us out with such a gift. That horse has already killed five men. It is well known from here to Penshurst.'

'It cannot be, for we have walked home together and he was as gentle as a lamb.' Maud was defiant.

'That may be. The devil plays many tricks.'

'You cannot believe this nonsense. It is superstition,' said Maud, her eyes pleading.

'Child, I know not what to believe. But our neighbours

11

will certainly believe. This horse will bring bad luck on this house.' His voice softened. 'Perhaps the curse can be broken.'

'Let me try, father. Give me a little time.'

Her father nodded, although reluctant. 'One week.'

The next morning, when all her early chores were done, Maud brought saddle and bridle to the stable where the black horse waited. 'You are truly beautiful,' she said. 'The monk had no name for you, merely calling you Black. For now, I too will call you Black. You are young, my Black. Our old Geoffrey will welcome the rest when you have replaced him.' She made to put the saddle on but the horse leapt away and turned his heels threateningly towards her. She wondered if the horse had ever been ridden.'This first time we will try without the saddle,' she said, slipping the halter over his head. 'I somehow think you will not take kindly to a bridle either.'

She led Black outside, his eyes rolling, his ears laid back. When he had calmed down, she grabbed a handful of mane and quick as lightning vaulted on to his broad back. The horse twisted into the air in a savage buck and within seconds Maud was back on the ground. Her father, watching from a distance, shook his head. 'You were warned. He's the devil's instrument.'

When Maud remounted she was ready for Black and stayed on for longer before he succeeded in throwing her. Each time she remounted, she became more determined and more prepared, and each time the horse became more determined to rid himself of this irritation.

So battle commenced and at the end of the week Maud, bruised and battered, was forced to admit defeat.

'What could have happened to make you so hate to be ridden?' she said, wiping Black's sweat-caked neck. The thought crossed her mind that the horse could indeed be cursed. But something deep inside her refused to accept this and she determined to try once more. Night was drawing on and rain was lashing at the stable door.

'One more chance, Black,' she whispered, remounting the startled horse. The door was open and the horse shot out into the night, Maud sitting his spine-jolting bucks and plunges. Black reared, and screeched a warning before turning suddenly and galloping towards the forest, leaping the stone wall that barred his path. Maud held her breath, her hands buried in the horse's mane, as they soared into the air. Black galloped on madly, his hooves churning the ground as he tried to outrun the wind and the rain. Maud's fear turned to exhilaration as they raced through the night, losing all track of time. The full moon loomed overhead, inviting them into her domain and Maud no longer cared if they were journeying into hell itself, so thrilling was the adventure. The forest became denser and overhanging branches threatened to dislodge her from the horse's back, scratching her face and neck. She did not notice the pain, only aware of the powerful force beneath her.

Then, without warning, she was falling, her head spinning, her thoughts blurred, and everything was still. When she came to, she thought for a minute that she was indeed in the devil's domain; all around her was dark and menacing. Then she saw Black standing nearby, his head low. He was resting a foreleg in an unnatural way and Maud slowly got to her feet, fighting dizziness.

'Whoa, Black, easy boy,' She put out her hand and gently ran it along the foreleg. A long cut stretched from the cannon bone down to the pastern.

'Poor Black,' she murmured. 'You must have caught it as you fell.' She tore a strip of cloth from her skirt and Black stood meekly while she bound the wound tightly.

'It looks like just a surface wound,' said Maud, leading

the horse up and down to prevent the leg stiffening. 'It should be bathed.' It did not take long to reach the river. She took a handkerchief and knelt by the riverbank, soaking it in the ice-cold water, in exactly the same place as the monk had knelt a week before. In her haste, she slipped on the mud and fell backwards into the treacherous waters.

Shocked, Maud went under, swallowing mouthfuls of the foul-tasting water. She strove to swim back to the bank but the current was too strong and pulled her back. She started to panic. She was alone; no-one would hear her cries for help. She had saved the monk from a watery grave: how ironic if she were to suffer the very fate he had avoided.

Suddenly the black horse was beside her, his huge bulk offering her safety, and she gripped his slippery mane as he swam back to the bank, defying the raging water. 'My brave horse,' she whispered.

When they had both recovered, the horse stood still while she mounted. He offered no resistance and they both knew the fight was over. 'You are not cursed,' said Maud. 'We are both blessed. I have a name for you now. I shall call you Lionheart.' She patted the horse's satin neck and he whinnied. 'Let's go home, Lionheart.'

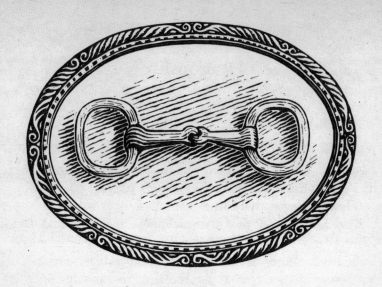

'Did I imagine what just happened?' Mo turned to her brother, her eyes wide.

'If you did then we're both going mad because I saw it too.'

They looked again at the picture.

'Mark – it's changed.'

'No it hasn't – a girl, a black horse, forest and . . . the river's not there. It's a road.'

'And the girl is dressed like me,' continued Mo.

'But look at the expression in that horse's eyes. They seem to . . . glow.'

Dragonsfire

Black thoroughbred gelding, 15.2hh, £900. Good home only. Cheryl gasped as John Kendall led out the magnificent horse that had been advertized in that evening's paper.

'Quite a brute,' her father commented.

The horse eyed them suspiciously, his ears laid flat. Cheryl tentatively patted his neck. How different he was from Danny, her last horse, quiet and patient. She felt a lump rise in her throat as she remembered how his life had ended, sprawled undignified and bloody on the road beside a battered car, while she had waited for the vet to arrive to relieve his agony. She swallowed and tried to banish these thoughts. That was six months ago. It was time to find a new focus. Another horse, her father had suggested.

'Better try him out, Cheryl,' she heard him say, and then to John, 'What do you call him?'

'Dragonsfire.'

John held the bridle as Cheryl mounted. The horse trembled beneath her and she was suddenly aware of his immense power and strength. She felt insignificant, weak, and hoped Dragonsfire would not sense this. She rode him round the paddock for a while and took him over a couple of low jumps before returning to her father.

'He moves beautifully. He looks quite a handful, though. Are you sure you can manage him?'

Cheryl avoided his gaze. 'I want him.'

She was surprised at how uncharacteristically definite she sounded. She knew she was a weak rider. She preferred a quiet understanding with animals and people; undemanding. She would win Dragonsfire with love and gentle handling. She could see it would not be easy.

'Well, if you are sure, and you seem to be,' said her father. He turned to John. 'Why is the price so low?'

John explained that he was selling the horse on behalf of friends whose daughter had died. Dragonsfire had belonged to her and understandably they no longer wanted the horse.

'I'll bring him over tomorrow,' said John and the sale was concluded.

In the early days of ownership Cheryl was delighted with Dragonsfire. He was too lively, perhaps, but an exciting ride. Her mother considered he was too strong for her – 'A man's horse', and admittedly he pulled sometimes. But gradually the occasional misdemeanour became the norm and Cheryl's confidence began to wane.

One morning events took a more sinister turn. She was grooming Dragonsfire in the stable, talking gently to him, still hoping to win his trust when she became aware that it was strangely silent. She stopped grooming and stared at the horse, surveying his powerful body. He turned to look at her with rolling eyes and suddenly she felt afraid. She started to back away. Dragonsfire moved towards her, blocking her exit.

Cheryl felt the wall behind her and pressed against it. Dragonsfire came nearer and she could feel his massive weight pushing her, crushing her against the cold stone. She started hitting him with her fists and shouting, until she became breathless and dizzy. As she lost consciousness she was aware of a heavy scent in the air, reminding her of flowers . . .

Cheryl avoided Dragonsfire for several days after this incident, trying to find explanations for what had happened. Perhaps she had unnerved the horse in some way that she was unaware of. She said nothing to her parents.

'That horse could do with some exercise,' her father said one morning.

'You've hardly been near him all week. Are you sure he's not too much for you? He needs a firm hand you know.'

'Yes, I do know.'

As Cheryl walked away her mother said, 'There's something about that horse, sort of . . . evil. I know that sounds silly. But he isn't doing Cheryl any good and she always was a nervous rider. She can't control him at all. I'm afraid they'll have an accident. Can't you do something?'

Her husband gave her a puzzled look.

'He's only a horse, dear, not some kind of monster. Cheryl needs her confidence building up. It would do her the world of good if she can master him.'

That night Cheryl awoke shivering from a nightmare about Dragonsfire. Rain beat against the window pane and images of the nightmare, the horse, flickered through her mind. She walked to the window and looked down at the stable. The moon shed an eerie light into the darkness and Cheryl thought she could see a shadowy figure standing outside the stable. She blinked and looked again. There *was* someone there. She pulled on a coat and boots and knocked on her parents' door.

'Dad, wake up, there's somebody in the yard.'

She ran down the stairs and outside while her parents, still half asleep, tried to rouse themselves.

Cheryl flashed a torch in the direction of the stable, wondering what its light would reveal. She entered nervously. Dragonsfire stared wide-eyed into the light, nostrils dilated. There was no mysterious companion with him.

'But I was sure I saw someone,' she said aloud. Suddenly

she felt ice-cold and the air became heavy with the scent of violets. Her father searched for some time in the yard and nearby, but no figure was sighted.

The following day Cheryl decided to pluck up her courage to ride again. As they trotted down the quiet country road she patted Dragonsfire's hard neck and thought how beautiful he was. She wished he was always as well-behaved as he was now. No sooner had she thought it than he began to toss his head, shaking the coarse dark hair. At first it was a gentle movement but soon he was shaking his head so violently that Cheryl became frightened. He was pulling the reins from her hands. She clung to the saddle and prayed he would not bolt. Instead, he began a series of bucks that quickly unseated Cheryl. After brief tears of frustration Cheryl began the walk home. Dragonsfire was nowhere to be seen.

She had not been walking long when a car drew up beside her. It was John Kendall.

'Want a lift?' Cheryl accepted gratefully. She soon found herself telling him of the problems she was having with Dragonsfire. 'Has he always been so difficult?' she asked.

John paused before speaking, as if choosing his words. 'His last owner was a girl your age; Miranda. The horse was really too strong for her. He was a headstrong beast. In fact, I'm surprised you still have him. But Miranda was devoted to him.' He laughed. 'Some people used to say he had an unhealthy influence on her. Before she died, as a result of a bad fall, she asked for the horse to be destroyed, so they could be together. Now that's what I call unhealthy; morbid even. Her parents never carried out this request which is why you have the dubious pleasure of owning Dragonsfire.'

When Cheryl arrived home she found that Dragonsfire had already returned and been stabled by her father. Her thoughts were uneasy and she wondered if it would be better to sell the horse after all. Why should she want to keep such a potentially dangerous creature, however beautiful? She decided to pay a visit to the Wilsons, parents of the tragic Miranda, to find out more about the horse. Mrs Wilson was pleased to have a visitor and happily showed Cheryl around their farm. 'Would you like to see some photographs of Miranda with Dragonsfire?' she offered. 'They're in her room.' As they neared the room Cheryl felt increasingly disturbed. The door opened and a sickly-sweet scent filled her nostrils. 'It's a lovely room,' began Mrs Wilson. 'And I always have fresh violets in here. They were Miranda's favourite flowers . . .' Her voice trailed off as she noticed Cheryl had slumped unconscious on the floor, her face ashen.

Several hours had elapsed before Cheryl recovered. She found herself back home and remembered that she had dreamed of Miranda confronting her, firmly telling her that she could not keep Dragonsfire. Miranda's emerald green eyes had transfixed her as she said; 'Dragonsfire belongs to me. I will never let you take him. Remember that.'

Cheryl shivered. She had never believed in ghosts. It must have been a dream. But she began to cry.

She rose early the next morning and went to the stables before her parents awoke. Dragonsfire stood away from her and she wished he would greet her with a whinny as her last horse, Danny, used to. It was foolish to hang on to Dragonsfire. He was making her life a misery. But part of her still wanted to possess his savage beauty, as Miranda had. Why should she be beaten?

Sadly, she acknowledged the fact that she had always been weak and lacking in willpower. If she could only summon up some courage and win for the first time in her life . . .

They took a winding path through the woods. The ground was still wet from the early morning mist. Cheryl started to relax. They were alone.

As they neared a clearing, a sweet perfume began to pervade the air. The glade was filled with violets. Cheryl could feel herself panicking and tried to pull Dragonsfire back, but it was too late. She could feel his whole body trembling with excitement. He emitted an unearthly scream then tore off at a gallop, with Cheryl clinging desperately to the reins.

It seemed as if they'd been racing for hours rather than minutes before Cheryl finally slipped from the saddle and hit the mossy ground. When she looked up, bruised and shaken, Dragonsfire was nowhere to be seen. But Cheryl was aware of a presence behind her. She turned. Miranda stood watching her, laughing.

'It isn't fair!' Cheryl heard herself shout, fear and anger in her voice. 'He's my horse now. Why can't you leave us alone?' She grabbed a handful of earth and threw it at the ghostly figure. Slowly it disappeared and all was again silent, except for the sound of Cheryl's sobs as she drifted into a deep sleep . . .

'. . . Cheryl, where have you been? We've been looking everywhere for you.' Cheryl's mother gave a sigh of relief as she walked towards the muddied figure standing by Dragonsfire. 'Sorry, Mum. We thought we'd have an early morning ride.' The girl patted Dragonsfire, who was nuzzling her affectionately.

'You seem to have made a breakthrough with that horse at last. He looks as if he's greeting a long-lost friend,' said Cheryl's mother. 'The morning air must have done you some good, too. You look invigorated. Let's go home for some breakfast.'

As they faded into the distance, the scent of violets faded too. A sad lone figure watched them. Tears wet Cheryl's face as she saw her mother greet the stranger as her daughter, while she herself was trapped in a body that did not belong to her, but to a dead world. She whispered her goodbyes to the beautiful black horse.

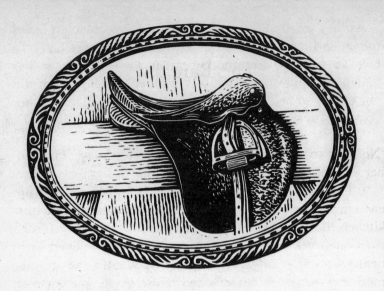

Mo shivered. 'What a strange coincidence.'

'What do you mean?' asked Mark.

'Well, in the first story, people thought the black horse was the devil, but of course, he wasn't really. In what we've just seen, the horse was evil, but no-one would believe it.'

'You're right. This is eerie. Let's see the next picture. I hope it's something more cheerful,' said Mark.

Mo looked wistfully at an image of a green field with no boundaries. It was occupied by a delicate chestnut mare with four white socks; a pale silver pony; and a flea-bitten grey with whiskers.

'That's the kind of picture I'd like on my wall. Then I could really believe we had ponies in our bedroom.'

Mark laughed. 'They'd make a terrible mess. Mum would go crazy!' But Mo was miles away, thinking about the ponies in the picture.

The Bargain

'No need to ask what Jo wants for her birthday,' laughed her younger brother.

'I'll probably be as old as granny before I've saved up enough to buy a pony,' groaned Jo, heading off to the kitchen to make tea.

In one week's time Jo would be thirteen. She lived with her ten-year-old brother, Robin, her parents and grandmother in a neat semi-detached house on the outskirts of a Lincolnshire market town. Although both her parents worked, there was little money left over for luxuries. When their grandmother had moved in a year previously, after the death of their grandfather, the household budget had to be stretched further and Jo lost all hope of ever being able to own a pony. She felt guilty at what she saw as selfish thoughts, particularly as she was fond of her grandmother.

The kettle boiled and Jo poured the steaming water into the teapot, poking the teabags with a spoon before pouring the brew into a cup. Her grandmother liked her tea black, with no sugar. Jo winced at the thought of the bitter taste. 'Here you are, gran,' she said. 'Do you want the telly on yet?'

'In a minute, dear. You are good to me, Jo. How much have you saved up so far to buy this pony, then?'

'One hundred and seventy three pounds, and twenty four pence.'

'Gosh, that's a lot of money,' said Robin, evidently impressed.

'But that took two whole years. There are so many other expenses; food, tack, stabling, vet's bills . . . the list is endless.' She sighed. 'It's time for that Australian serial to start. I'll put the telly on.'

'Happy birthday, Jo,' her family chorused when she appeared at breakfast.

'How does it feel to be a teenager, then?' asked her mother, hugging her.

'Much the same as being twelve,' laughed Jo.

'Open your presents, then,' demanded Robin.

Jo carefully opened the blue envelope from her parents. Inside was a card with a horse on the front and by the greeting they had written 'WE OWE YOU SIX RIDING LESSONS.'

'But that's an awful lot of money,' she protested.

'Nonsense. You deserve it. You always work for rides down at that riding centre. Now you'll be a paying customer for a change.'

'Thanks. It's a lovely present.'

'Now open mine.' Robin handed her a small parcel. Through the flimsy paper Jo could tell immediately that it was a book.

'It's about keeping a horse,' said Robin before she had torn open the wrapping.

'That's lovely, Robin, thank you,' said Jo, though inside she felt a twinge of sadness, knowing she would be unlikely to be able to put into practice what she learned from the book.

Her grandmother was quiet, studying Jo's face, guessing what she was thinking.

'There is only one thing to make Jo's birthday perfect,' she said. 'Come over here, Jo.' She pressed a paper bundle into her granddaughter's hand.

Jo opened her hand and gasped as she counted the fifty-pound notes.

'Six hundred pounds! But Gran, you can't possibly afford that!'

'Don't go telling me what I can and can't afford, young lady. Your grandfather left behind a little money when he died.'

Jo clasped the bundle tightly. 'I don't know what to say.'

'You don't have to say anything. Just make sure you choose a nice pony. Now, about its keep. Until you get a part-time job, I will pay for everything. When you are able to do this, I will still pay out any extra bills, like the vet or the blacksmith.'

'Your grandmother has arranged for a place to keep the pony, too,' said Jo's mother. 'Mr Wilson has a field to rent, with a stable. He only lives a mile away so it won't take you long to cycle there every day.'

'Mr Wilson is an old friend of mine. He has agreed to let the field for a very low rent,' said her grandmother.

'Thank you so much, everybody. Now all I have to do is find a pony!'

'What about this one? "Palomino mare, 13.2hh, lovely temperament. £650 or near offer." She sounds nice,' said Robin, waving the newspaper under Jo's nose.

'We haven't got £650, though,' replied Jo.

'But we could beat them down in price.'

'But we might not, and then it would be a waste of everyone's time. Anyway, I want to get a bargain, if I can. That way, the spare money can be used to buy any extra things I might need,' said Jo.

She put her pen down. 'Well, I've made a list of four possible ponies. We'd better make a start.'

She made the necessary phone calls to arrange to look

at the ponies, and her father agreed to drive her to view them. 'We'll be looking at two this evening and two tomorrow,' she said to Robin.

'Can I come too?' he asked.

'Only if you promise to behave.'

The first pony lived a few miles away and had been described as a five year old chestnut mare of fourteen hands with a sweet nature. As their car drew up the long driveway Jo saw at least a dozen horses and ponies in an adjacent field and a large stable block.

'This is a big house,' commented Robin. 'And he's got a tennis court. I bet the owner must be rich.'

A tall well-dressed man answered the door, flanked by two greyhounds. He extended a hand adorned with large rings to Jo's father.

'Good day to you, sir. A pleasant day it is, too. This is the young lady, is it?' He turned to Jo. 'I have a delightful pony, just right for you. She's all tacked up, ready and waiting!'

They followed him towards the stable where a groom was holding a pretty chestnut pony with four white socks and a tiny circle of white hairs on her forehead.

'She's beautiful,' agreed Jo.

'Her name is Juniper. I'm sure you can't wait to try her out.' He gestured to the groom to give her a leg up and opened the gate to a small paddock.

'I have put up a few jumps for you.'

Juniper seemed very responsive to Jo's aids and trotted out neatly. Although a little inexperienced, Jo was a careful and precise rider. When she returned to the stable her face was flushed with pleasure.

'She's lovely. She jumps well, too, if a bit hesitant.'

'Like I said, a perfect first pony; gentle as a kitten. She has Arab blood in her; look at that dish face.'

'What price are you asking again?' asked Jo's father.

'Seven hundred . . .'

'But I thought you said on the phone . . .'

'. . . but because the little lady has fallen in love with the pony, six hundred.' Jo looked astonished.

'What do you think, Jo?' asked her father. 'You do like her, don't you?'

'She's wonderful. But I had hoped to have a bit spare for the tack. Still, I . . .'

'Tell you what, I'll throw in the tack at no extra cost and that's a bargain.'

'Don't you think you ought at least to look at the other ponies first?' queried Jo's father. 'You shouldn't make any hasty decisions.'

'There are plenty of people queueing up to buy this mare,' said the owner, his voice becoming sharp. 'It's only because I've taken a liking to the lady that I'm prepared to reduce the price.' He smiled. 'My priority is to find Juniper a good home, not to make money.'

'I want this pony, Dad. I'm certain.' Jo was adamant.

'Alright. You know best. I'll make the arrangements.'

Juniper was indeed everything the man had promised and Jo was delighted she had managed to get such a bargain. The mare seemed to take a long while to settle in her new field and she tended to be nervous with strangers but she had the gentlest nature and soon the whole family had fallen for her. She would follow Jo round the field like a dog and when she was feeling sleepy she loved to lean her head on Jo's shoulder and doze.

They would go for long leisurely hacks together down the lanes and through the woods, usually taking the same route. Occasionally they would have to cross over a busy road, which would make Juniper nervous, and she would shy and jump at the slightest sound.

'I don't think she can have been schooled in traffic,' said Jo to her father. 'Either that or she's had a bad experience on the road sometime in the past.'

'Be careful, Jo. Don't take any risks,' warned her father.

'I won't. But she has to learn how to cope with traffic.'

The following morning Jo decided to go for a short ride before lunch. It had been a rainy week and since the weather was unexpectedly fine she wanted to take advantage of the sun. Juniper greeted her with a whinny as Jo's feet crunched on the gravel and she whistled to her. At least Juniper is easy to catch and tack up, thought Jo as she fetched the saddle and bridle from the stable.

They took their usual route across the common for a gallop and then walked through the woods before crossing a junction and coming back up a quiet side road. Jo was daydreaming, her mind occupied with thoughts of entering Juniper for the open jumping class at the next local show, when a car pulled out and overtook them too fast, narrowly missing Juniper and driving through a large puddle, splashing the mare with water. Startled, Juniper shot forward, straight into a parked car. She squealed with pain and reared up, throwing Jo into a ditch. Jo recovered quickly and rushed over to her pony. Juniper stood resting her foreleg awkwardly and Jo saw at once that it was cut.

'Oh Juniper, you poor thing. Stay still, now, while I bandage you up with my scarf.'

The walk back seemed to take forever. Mr Wilson was digging his garden when they returned, and looked up as he heard hoofbeats.

'You stay with her, Jo, while I call the vet and your father,' he said throwing down his spade.

It was half an hour before the vet arrived by which

time Juniper was feeling very sorry for herself, despite Jo's attempts to soothe her.

When the vet had examined her leg he said, 'It's not as bad as it looks. She'll be fine, don't worry, although her leg will be a bit sore for a while. No riding for a fortnight, to be certain.' He patted the mare. 'She's a lovely pony, is Juniper. I'm glad she's found a good home.'

'You know her, then?' asked Jo in surprise.

'Oh, yes. I treated her a year ago. Not easy to find a home for a blind pony.'

There was a stunned silence.

'What did you say?' Jo was incredulous.

'Surely you knew? This pony has a degenerative disease of the eye. It was in the early stages last year so I reckon that by now she will be almost completely blind.'

'We have only had Juniper for three months. No one told us.' Jo said slowly, running her fingers through the pony's mane. 'I suppose it explains a few things, though.'

'What does this mean, then, for Jo? Is the pony safe?' asked her father, concern in his voice.

'I wouldn't advise jumping, but the pony will be fine for quiet hacking, on familiar routes. Best to steer clear of roads, though. She's in no pain and perfectly healthy otherwise,' replied the vet. 'There is one other thing you ought to know, if you don't already. How long did you say you have had the pony? Three months?'

Jo nodded.

'Unless I'm very much mistaken, Juniper is in foal. I can do some tests but I'm sure they will confirm it.'

'It looks to me like her last owner saw a blind and pregnant pony to be something of a liability. He must have thought we were right fools,' said Jo's father.

'I wouldn't say that,' replied the vet as he watched Jo hugging Juniper. 'Not only have you got a delightful, sweet-

31

natured pony but with any luck you will soon be the proud owners of a healthy foal. Two for the price of one.' He smiled. 'I would say that *is* something of a bargain.'

Horse Thief

Caron crouched down low behind the hedge. She had been watching the house for nearly a fortnight now and she was getting to learn the habits of its occupants. More importantly, to Caron, she knew when the stables were left unattended. At night an Alsatian roamed the yard, so she would have to choose her moment carefully. She did not want to antagonize the dog unneccessarily.

The house was large, well-maintained and Caron was certain the owners did not have to worry about money as she did. She had not seen a man about the place but assumed he worked in the city all week.

'Probably a stockbroker,' she told herself. 'They must be rolling in money.'

She had often seen a woman in the garden, pottering around, and a girl of about fourteen, her own age.

But what interested Caron most of all was the girl's pony.

He was neat and dainty, a Welsh-Arab cross, the colour of pale silver. He moved like a dancer, his banner of a tail streaming out behind him, his head held high, giving him a haughty manner. He reminded her so much of her own lost pony, Midi, that she could almost believe he was Midi. But Midi was gone. Caron felt her eyes water as the last day with her beloved pony flashed before her. She saw him being loaded into the horsebox, ears pricked as he walked up the ramp, expecting to be driven to another horse show.

She saw the man who had bought him writing out the cheque and handing it to her mother.

'Judas,' she had thought bitterly.

But most of all she remembered the sound of her pony whinnying as the horsebox drove away, the sound echoing in her head. She had covered her ears in a desperate attempt to shut out the sound, but she could never shut it out; it would always be with her. Even though a year had passed she could hear it as clearly as if it were yesterday. She could only hope that Midi's new owner would care for him as she had.

She had hated them all; the man who had just bought Midi, her mother, even the driver of the horsebox. Most of all she hated her father for walking out on them, leaving them with little enough money to support themselves, let alone a pony.

Caron looked again at the grey pony, Midi's doppel-ganger. She had planned what she would do; had been planning it for days. They would take off to the hills and live off the land; they would be free.

It was half-light. The pony was standing in the yard, tethered to a fence while the girl groomed him. She brushed energetically, whistling as she worked. She was a petite girl, almost frail; fair-skinned with blue eyes, light blonde hair and a pretty face.

Caron felt overwhelmingly jealous. The girl had looks, a smart house and a pony. It didn't seen fair. Why should some people have everything?

Just then the woman called from the house, 'Phone call, Francesca.' The girl stopped grooming and rushed away.

For a moment Caron did not move. She could not quite believe this unexpected stroke of luck. Then, seeing her chance, she ran over to the pony, untied the rope and took him hurriedly into the woods that flanked the house.

'That was easy,' she told the pony, surprise in her voice. He nibbled at her sleeve, hoping for titbits. She laughed, rubbing the soft down of his muzzle. 'So like my Midi,' she whispered. 'Now we must go.'

She gestured to the house. 'She won't miss you. She can buy another pony. I'm sure her parents can afford it.'

Her words were assured but deep inside her conscience stirred.

When they reached the hills Caron vaulted on to the pony's back. This was the moment she had waited so long for. She squeezed her legs against the pony's sides and they were off, cantering, then galloping across the open expanse of land. Caron felt that a long lost friend had been returned. The wind whistled past her ears and across her eyes, making them water. She crouched over the pony's neck, revelling in the speed and freedom, forgetting all sense of time. She forgot their tiny council flat, the queues in the social security office, the unpaid bills and her mother's sad eyes. All that mattered now was having a pony again.

Finally they stopped and Caron, hot and sweating, dismounted and walked the pony to cool him off.

They spent the night in an old shepherd's hut she had discovered weeks before. It was colder than Caron had expected and she snuggled up against the pony for warmth. She awoke at five, hungry and thirsty and reached into her rucksack for sandwiches and Coke. The pony lay his head on her shoulder, dribbling and Caron shared her last sandwich with him. For the first time in a year she felt happy. Pulling her jacket tightly around her, she drifted off into a contented sleep.

At seven thirty Caron stretched and yawned before venturing out of the hut to greet the day. She had barely got out of the hut when a voice said, 'I've come for my pony.' The girl stared straight at Caron, her eyes daggers.

Caron was taken aback. 'How did you find me?' She began to feel nervous.

'I've been watching you skulking around. You think I didn't notice? Not a very good thief, are you. I followed the tracks. I never imagined it was my pony you were after.' The girl's face was strained and taut. 'Now, give him back.'

Suddenly Caron felt indignant. 'Why should I? Anyway, your parents can buy you another pony.'

'You think so?'

The girl's voice changed. 'Please give him back.' Suddenly she looked vulnerable and Caron noticed dark rings under her eyes due to lack of sleep. Her eyes were red and swollen.

'He's all I've got. He means the world to me,' said the girl and Caron thought she was going to break down and cry.

Caron was about to repeat, 'Why should I?' but held back. She was beginning to feel uncomfortable.

The girl looked away. 'Won't your mother be worried about you?' she asked. 'Or is she the sort of mother who doesn't care about her kids? Maybe that's why you're a delinquent. Maybe I'll end up like you one day.'

Caron was furious. 'How dare you! Of course my mum cares about me!'

'Aren't you the lucky one,' the girl said coldly. 'My mother wrapped me in a dustbin liner and dumped me on the steps of a hospital when I was two days old. Or so I was told.'

'But I thought . . .' Caron's voice trailed off.

'That woman you saw in the garden; that's Rosa. She adopted me when I was twelve.'

Caron felt unsettled. Things were not turning out as she had imagined.

'I was brought up in a children's home; had a string of foster parents,' continued the girl. 'Rosa is the first person who wanted to adopt me officially.'

'What's she like? She has a great house. She must have plenty of money,' said Caron.

'She does alright. Her husband spends most of his time working in Saudi Arabia. He only comes home for holidays. I think Rosa really cares about me but she's not very emotional. She doesn't show it. We argue a lot. I suppose we don't have much in common.'

'What about the pony – he is yours?'

'Oh yes. Jubilee. Rosa bought him for my thirteenth birthday.' Her eyes misted over. 'Jubilee is a different matter. He doesn't pick fights or make fun of me like the kids at school. He doesn't criticize because I can't do my school work. He didn't abandon me.' She looked away and wiped her sleeve across her eyes, hoping Caron wouldn't see. 'Jubilee is my only friend; the only thing I ever loved.'

Caron could not face the girl, her guilt too much to cope with. Suddenly her own problems paled into insignificance. How could she have known, she told herself. But it doesn't matter; she should never have taken the pony in the first place. He did not belong to her. She had broken the law, stolen a pony. The word 'Thief' flashed across her mind and she felt suddenly afraid.

She went into the hut and led the pony out. He was not Midi, but Jubilee. She took the halter rope and offered it to the girl.

'I don't know what to say,' Caron mumbled. 'I'm sorry.'

The girl smiled nervously. 'Thank you.'

'I suppose you called the police,' said Caron.

'No.'

'Why not?'

'I don't know really. I was curious about you, wondered why you took Jubilee, why you were watching.'

Suddenly Caron found herself telling the girl about Midi and her father leaving, pouring out her heart as the girl had done.

'We were an ordinary average family,' said Caron. 'Not well off or anything, but we managed.'

'Things are never what they seem,' said the girl. 'Look, I don't even know your name. I'm Francesca, but I hate that name, so call me Chez.'

'I'm Caron.'

Unnoticed by the girls it had started to rain, and Jubilee began to fidget, impatient to get back to his warm stable.

'We'd better go back,' said Caron. 'Your pony must be hungry.'

'We can't leave things like this,' said Chez anxiously. 'I think we should search for Midi and buy him back. Your mother must have the address of the man who bought him.'

Caron looked downcast. 'It's a year since he was sold and the man was a dealer. Midi could be anywhere.'

But Chez was adamant. 'Don't be so defeatist. You can't abandon him. With a little detective work we can track him down. It's been done before.'

'But I haven't any money,' said Caron.

'Rosa has. I'll get her to buy him. He can live with us, keep Jubilee company. And we can ride together.'

Her eyes were shining and Caron became infected with her enthusiasm.

'But what if we can't find him? What if . . . ?'

'It can be done somehow, we must never give up hope.'

They walked down the hill in the rain, talking about the future and Caron realized that she had something to live for again.

Fluke

'It's a nice old place. What do you think, Katy?'

Katy looked up at her father, a blank expression on her face, then turned her eyes to the stark cottage hewn from rough grey stone. She couldn't bring herself to speak, the memory of their comfortable little semi-detached house fresh in her mind. It had always been warm there, on the coast, their home bright and welcoming, filled with her mother's presence.

'It's cold here,' she said.

Her father surveyed the bleak moorland. 'Let's get inside quickly, then.' He took his daughter's hand.

The went in, their boots heavy with farmyard mud.

'We'd better leave them by the door,' said her father, almost whispering, as if he somehow expected the cottage to be occupied. The air smelt musty and damp. 'Better get this fire going. Find the kettle, will you, Katy, and make us some coffee.'

Katy put down her suitcase and wandered into the tiny kitchen. There was a small gas cooker, a camping fridge at the bottom of the pantry and a stainless steel sink and drainer. She filled the kettle with water, hunted through the cupboards to see what crockery was provided for them and stared through the window at the dreary landscape. Then she thought of her mother and started to cry.

Katy Barclay was twelve, a frail and timid girl, made more so by the sudden death of her mother from a rare illness. After the funeral her father had immersed himself in his work, unable to cope with his bereavement and Katy had been looked after by various relatives. Feeling isolated, Katy suffered an emotional trauma and her father eventually gave up his job to care for her. Unable to support their expensive house, Mr Barclay had sold up, taken up writing as a career and rented a farm cottage on the Yorkshire moors.

'You won't need to go to school until you feel ready,' Mr Barclay had said. 'I can teach you at home. We'll be all right, Katy.'

The rain drizzled down outside and Katy remembered that she was supposed to be making coffee.

Katy spent most of the week in the cottage, unable to settle to anything for long. She gazed through the window while her father worked at his desk. Her aunt had given her a rug making kit, which occupied her for brief periods and she read seemingly endless women's magazines supplied by Mrs Weeks, the wife of the farmer who let their cottage.

'I'll get you a portable television from the town next time I go,' said her father one day. 'I'll get a word processor too. Every writer needs a word processor.'

When she got completely bored inside the cottage Katy eventually ventured out for a walk.

'Fresh air. That's what you need,' called Mr Weeks as he looked up from repairing a fence. 'I'll show you round the farm, if you like.'

Although she was not very interested in the farm Katy agreed, telling herself it would at least be something to do.

'What animals do you keep?' she asked, without enthusiasm.

'Pigs, mostly,' replied Mr Weeks. 'And a cat or two.'

They toured the pigsty, and Katy was introduced to the pigs, who all had names. Crossing the yard to the farm-

44

house for coffee Katy noticed a stable tucked away behind the woodshed.

Mr Weeks followed her gaze.

'Oh, that's old Fluke.'

'A pony?'

'Do you want to see him?'

Katy nodded. 'I like horses.'

As they approached Fluke put his head over the half-door. He was a flea-bitten grey with a long forelock and whiskers.

'That's old Fluke. Must be getting on twenty now.'

Katy rubbed her fingertips on Fluke's pink muzzle and the pony thrust his head forward to explore her pockets.

'He's a greedy devil,' laughed Mr Weeks.

'He's lovely,' said Katy.

'Past his best, but we all have to get old. Now don't go getting too attached to him.'

But Katy ignored his warning and over the next few weeks, spending time with Fluke became a habit. At first she would visit him in the mornings and stroke him and chat to him. Then she came over in the afternoons with titbits and Mrs Weeks gave her a dandy brush to groom him. Katy enjoyed her time with Fluke and he returned her affection.

'You look a lot more cheerful these days,' commented her father, evidently pleased. He had noticed that his daughter was becoming less dependent on him, and brooded far less about her mother.

'Maybe you'll be able to go back to school in September,'

'Maybe,' said Katy, putting the finishing touches to her rug.

She was mucking out Fluke's stable when Mr Weeks shattered her hopes.

'He's going, Katy. I can't afford to keep him any longer. He's too old to work any more.'

Katy froze. 'You can't mean it.'

'I did warn you. It was only a matter of time. You can't ride him. He's got a weak back. He's old.'

'I know. But how can you sell him?'

Mr Weeks looked away. 'I wasn't going to sell him, Katy, love.'

An atmosphere of doom hung over the cottage the following day. A lorry collected Fluke just before lunch, closely followed by the dustman and his lorry. This seemed strangely ironic. Kate couldn't bear to say goodbye to Fluke but she watched the lorry leave as the dustman arrived. She saw Mrs Weeks greet the dustman and invite him in for a cup of tea.

Katy went up to her bedroom and leant on the window sill, scraping at the peeling paint on the frames. Suddenly she became aware of a noise in the yard. One of the piglets had escaped from the pigsty and was sniffing around the rubbish bags. She watched him for a while but her mind wandered to thoughts of Fluke and his fate so she soon lost interest in the piglet.

Finally the dustman came out, sealed the rubbish bags and threw them into the dustcart. As he climbed into the cab to operate the machinery to close the doors Katy heard a sound, a high pitched squeak that seemed to come from inside the cart. The piglet was nowhere to be seen and a horrifying thought struck her. Within seconds she had rushed downstairs and outside, yelling at the dustman. He had closed the doors and was preparing to go.

'Stop, stop, there's a piglet trapped!' she yelled above the noise of the engine. The dustman looked bemused but she finally convinced him to open the back of the dustcart. He pulled out the rubbish bags and opened them and to his surprise found an anxious piglet inside, squealing in protest.

'You were right,' said the dustman in amazement.

'Whatever is going on out here?' said Mrs Weeks, joining them. 'I heard such a commotion.'

Once the incident had been cleared up and Katy had been thanked, everything else seemed like an anti-climax.

'You need to get out, Katy,' said her father after lunch. 'We both do.'

They spent the afternoon in town and Katy's father bought her a blouse and a smart fountain pen to cheer her up. They had dinner in a restaurant and went to the cinema afterwards to see a comedy before returning home. Katy felt too tired to brood.

She slept late and her father brought her breakfast in bed.

'I know it's been tough, Katy, but let's make a fresh start. We'll be all right.' The sun shone through the curtains, the first really fine day since they had been in the cottage. Katy hoped it was an omen and determined to accept the way things were.

The yard looked cleaner that usual and the cats yawned and stretched on the roof of the woodshed. Katy's eye caught the stable and she felt drawn towards it. Part of her hoped for a miracle as she peered inside but the stable was empty. Sighing, she turned away and came face to face with Mr Weeks.

'Morning, Katy. We have a guest to stay. Bring him in, Jeff.'

Katy's eyes widened as Fluke was led out of a horsebox.

'He's back. But I thought . . .'

'I'm obliged to you for saving my piglet. Valuable, he is. So Mrs Weeks had a strong word with me, reckoned I owed you something, reckoned I was getting too concerned

47

with things earning their keep.' He blushed. 'So it seems we'll be keeping old Fluke for a good while yet, you'll be glad to hear.'

'It was a bit of luck then, me seeing that piglet,' said Katy. For the first time since arriving at the cottage she laughed. 'I suppose you might call it a fluke.'

'This is thirsty work. Let's go and find a coffee bar,' said Mo. It took a little while for their eyes to adjust to the light outside after the darkness of the gallery. They crossed the road and headed for a local café.

It was lunchtime and the place was crowded.

'Is that seat taken?'

They looked up to see an elderly man with wrinkled face and gnarled hands clutching a mug of tea. Mark shook his head. 'Do sit down.'

The man smiled a toothless smile and Mark thought he must be at least a hundred.

'Cold day,' said the man, rubbing his hands.

'Yes,' agreed Mo.

There was a silence for a while as all three of them stared out of the window at the cars rushing past.

'Of course, in my day, us working folks couldn't afford to buy cars.'

Progress

Dawn was breaking in Norwich. It was 1910. A middle-aged man and his young son were going about their morning routine.

'Come on, lad. Better get Polly ready. Our customers will be waiting.'

Polly was an elderly skewbald cob who had been with the family for as long as William Baxter could remember. Her sweet, gentle nature made her popular with the people they delivered bread to and her distinctive colour made her instantly recognizable. She was the only coloured pony in the district. Her hard feet and strong legs made her reliable for working on rough roads.

'Good day to you, William,' said Mrs Jordan, a chatty customer who often complained about the weather. She made a fuss of Polly, feeding her crusts and stale buns.

'She's a real lady, William. Not like the coalman's horse. She lays her ears back whenever anyone comes near her,' she confided before proceeding to gossip to William's father about her neighbours.

When their round had finished Polly headed for home, ignoring the noise of the occasional motor car, but nervous of the strong petrol smells.

'She's a good ol' gel. Those poor London horses have a terrible time with all that traffic stopping and starting, and now these electric motor cabs scaring them to death. There'll be chaos in the streets there before long, I shouldn't wonder.'

'Uncle Ted says the horses on the omnibus only give half the service they did fifty years ago, the strain is that bad. They mainly use Canadian horses now you know. They cost thirty pounds too.'

'Your Uncle Ted can keep London, as far as I'm concerned. Give me Norwich any day.'

When they got back, William's mother had prepared tea and they toasted bread in front of the coal fire. They lived on the upper floor of a terraced house, with the bakery on the ground floor. Their house had recently been converted to electric lighting and it was a cosy place, with pictures on the wall and china ornaments cluttering the mantel. They were the first people in the street to have wallpaper.

'Do you know that Elsie Swansdyke's daughter has bought a bicycle! I don't know what the world's coming to,' exclaimed William's mother.

Her husband laughed. 'Riding a bicycle is all the thing now, especially for the ladies. Still, cycles are not too popular with a lot of people, since cyclists don't have to pay road tax.'

'I don't care if it is the fashion. And she had the gall to complain of motor cars splashing her and forcing her into the gutter. I told her she was only fit for the gutter.'

'Times are changing, Nelly. We all have to move with the times,' said Mr Baxter.

The next day, after William had completed the early round, he arrived home to find his parents discussing the contents of a letter that had just been delivered. He could tell by their faces that something had happened.

'Well, son, we have had good news as a result of your Aunt Agatha leaving this world. Not that we aren't sad at her unfortunate demise,' he hastened to add. '. . . though we hardly knew her.'

'God rest her soul. She had a good innings,' his mother

said, lowering her voice. 'But she has left us a windfall. A considerable sum of money. Two hundred pounds.'

'We have to decide what to do with it,' said Mr Baxter. 'There are lots of things we could do with, like a bathroom, piped water supply and an electric cooker.'

'We could even afford a housemaid,' said his wife, quickly warming to the idea.

'Or a good school for William.'

For the rest of the day William's head was spinning, full of ideas for what to do with their new-found wealth.

His father was also preoccupied. 'I have been looking into the matter, William. A new twin cyclinder van will cost £150. Of course, there are extra costs and the tyres are expensive. But the fuel is very cheap.'

'But what about Polly? What will happen to her if we get a van?' asked William. Mr Baxter stared ahead, unwilling to answer.

The benefits of replacing Polly with a van were discussed over tea.

'Old Mr Simpson will have to give up his bread round, due to his bad back, so rumour has it,' William's mother informed them between mouthfuls of buttered scone. 'You know what that could mean?'

'Yes, that devil Bert Arkwright will move in and take over the round with his bread van. Unless we had a van, too,' said Mr Baxter. 'A van could do twice the work of Polly. It would be a good investment.'

'She's twenty-four now. She deserves a rest.'

'So we can retire her, then?' asked William.

'Not exactly, William,' Mr Baxter said awkwardly. 'We can't really afford to keep her and the van. We'll need all the extra money to buy the fuel and look after it.'

William's face fell.

'She's not a pet, dear, although we're all very fond of her. She's a working animal,' his mother said gently.

'You have to be businesslike to get on in this world,' Mr Baxter added.

Two weeks later their motor van arrived. Brimming with pride, William's father immediately polished up the already gleaming paintwork before proceeding to load up for the first delivery.

Polly thrust her head over the stable door, curious at the newcomer, her nostrils twitching as she took in the strange smells of oil and polish. With everyone's attention on the new van her feed was late and she signalled her disapproval by banging the stable door.

'Sorry, Polly, just coming.' William attended to his morning duties and after she had been fed and groomed Polly waited patiently for William to fetch her harness. To her surprise he merely patted her neck, turned her into the paddock and joined his father in the van.

'We'll hang on to Polly for a little while, just to make sure the van is all right,' explained Mr Baxter. 'Then we'll make some changes to the stable. We could do with somewhere to keep the van.'

The van ran more smoothly and quietly than William had expected. His memories were of the early cars that snorted and shook and were less than reliable. Mr Baxter was well satisfied with his purchase, although not all his customers shared his enthusiasm.

'I don't hold with horseless carriages,' complained Mrs Jordan. 'They're not human.'

'But then neither is Polly,' pointed out Mr Baxter, winking at William, ' – and the van is much more efficient. You'll get your bread even earlier.'

'That's not the point. I look forward to saying hello to

Polly. I save up crusts for her. I'm sure you will find that a lot of your customers will miss her.'

Despite the misgivings of a number of his customers, William's father was confident of the advantages of the van. When Mr Simpson gave up his round due to ill-health he took that on too, much to the annoyance of his rival, Bert Arkwright.

'It will mean a lot of extra work, but more money of course,' Mr Baxter told his family.

But William was missing Polly's company, missing the people she attracted over for a chat, most of whom were not interested in making conversation by the motor van. He looked wistfully at the horse's straw hat gathering dust by the door. It had been given to her by an affectionate customer who hated to see her bothered by the summer flies.

Shortly after taking on the extra round, the van began to play up.

On an exceptionally hot day, when they were pulling up a steep hill, steam began to pour out of the engine and the van spluttered a loud protest before grinding to a halt.

'Blast. What can be wrong?' said Mr Baxter, getting out to investigate. 'I don't know a thing about these motors.'

'How are we going to get this bread delivered if we can't get the van going?' asked William. 'Arkwright will poach our territory if we don't turn up.'

'You're right, William. We can't afford to lose this new round.'

'It will take me about an hour to run home from here and fetch Polly and the van. We can at least salvage some of the day.'

'I'd better go to the nearest garage,' said Mr Baxter.

Just then, the sound of a bell ringing loudly distracted them from their problems.

It was a girl of about sixteen, her long auburn hair blowing in the wind, riding a bicycle.

'Goodness, it's Elsie Swansdyke's girl, Emmy. On one of those bicycles your mother hates so much,' grinned Mr Baxter. 'Good day, Emmy.'

'Having trouble, Mr Baxter?'

She threw her bicycle down by the hedge and strode over in a manner that William's mother would have thought most unladylike.

Ignoring William, who was staring open-mouthed, she bent over the engine.

'It's overheated, hasn't it?' she said.

'How would you know that?' William asked, unable to conceal his amazement.

'What, you mean because I'm a girl? I suppose you think girls shouldn't know these things,' she said disdainfully. Without giving him a chance to reply she continued, 'My dad knows all about motor cars. He was one of the first people to own one. We got some money, see,' she said, leaning over confidentially.

'That's right, I heard he had two cars now.'

'Oh yes, he teaches me about how to fix them. I'm going to be a car mechanic.' Emmy said proudly. 'Mind you, it's probably better if Dad fixed this one. We'd need to get it home though.'

'There's a farmer lives just down the road,' said Mr Baxter. 'He's got a couple of old Shires. I'm sure he wouldn't mind lending them for an hour or two to tow this van.'

'What about your round, though? How are you going to finish it?' asked Emmy.

'I'm going to fetch Polly,' replied William.

'But it will take you a good hour to get back if you walk,'

said Emmy. 'I know – you can borrow my bicycle. It'll be much quicker.'

William blushed. 'I've hardly ridden a bicycle. Are you sure you don't mind?'

'Of course not. Off you go now.'

William sat awkwardly on the seat and as the bicycle wobbled down the hill, he could hear Emmy laughing.

Polly was pleased to see him back home and waited patiently for him to put the harness on and get the cart ready.

As they trotted off down the street, William couldn't resist a wry smile as he remembered the shocked reaction of his mother when he told her about Emmy Swansdyke, although she admitted she was grateful for the girl's help. Their old customers were glad to see Polly working again, and after her rest she was friskier than ever. She was deluged with gifts of carrots and buns and lapped up all the attention and fuss.

Mr Baxter arrived home later that evening, looking tired and anxious.

'Mr Swansdyke will fix the van for us, but it will cost. Worst of all, the van won't be ready until tomorrow. He's not sure when, but he thinks he can do it by lunchtime.'

'Me and Polly can do the morning round, then,' said William, secretly pleased.

'I bet you're glad you kept Polly, eh Dad?'

'Of course, lad. But we can't afford to make this a habit.'

As soon as the van was back on the road, Polly was put out to pasture and Mr Baxter started to make arrangements to sell her at the market. But Bert Arkwright had quickly taken advantage of his rival's misfortune and had already poached some of the Baxter's customers. If the two of them met in the street, harsh words were bandied. Mr Baxter decided to stoop to more devious measures to get his customers back and started a rumour that Arkwright was selling stale bread. A war ensued and William was relieved when, on a particularly busy morning, his mother asked him to stay at home and help her in the bakery.

But his relief was short-lived. Only half an hour after his father had left, there was a loud knock on the door. It was Mrs Jordan.

'How nice to see you, Mrs Jordan,' said Mrs Baxter, ushering her in. 'How are the children?'

'I'm afraid this is not a social visit, Mrs Baxter. Your poor husband asked me to come. He had just delivered to number three and was getting in the van when he noticed the tyres had been let down. He's stranded at present.'

'It was that rogue, Arkwright, I'll be bound,' said Mrs Baxter, her eyes narrowing.

'He wants William to finish the round with Polly,' Mrs Jordan leaned back in her chair to catch her breath.

'That long walk must have been thirsty work, Mrs Jordan. I'll make a pot of tea. Off you go, William. I can manage here,' said Mrs Baxter.

Polly trotted to the fence when she saw William.

'We're off again, old girl,' he said. 'Horse to the rescue.' He had loaded the bread and was just about to climb into the driver's seat when he heard a scream from the house. He ran inside to see broken china and water strewn over the kitchen floor.

'Whatever happened?' he asked.

'Nothing, William, just dropped the teapot. Made us jump a bit, that's all,' replied his mother. 'No need to make a fuss.'

'Best get on, William,' said Mrs Jordan.

But when he went back outside Polly had gone.

'Oh no, that's all we need,' groaned William. 'With our luck, Arkwright has probably stolen her.'

Rolling up his sleeves, he set off in pursuit, wondering how he could tell his father. 'We're sure to lose our round, now.'

As he approached Tipton Road he noticed a familiar figure in the distance. 'Hello, Emmy,' he said.

'Good day to you, William Baxter. What's up with you? You've got a face as long as a poker.'

'So would you if your horse had just been stolen,' he replied.

'Really? But I've just seen Polly down the next street. If you hurry, you'll catch up with her.' With a laugh she cycled away.

Despite being tired and hot, William ran on. Rounding the corner, he passed Jack Watson, a long-standing customer, who said, 'Glad to see old Pol is back on the rounds again.'

At the end of the street, William could just make out the skewbald cob, plodding from house to house, stopping for the customers to come out and waiting longer for those elderly people who had trouble getting about. Curious, William followed at a distance.

When she had completed the round, Polly turned and headed for home.

William gave her an extra feed that night.

Over supper, Mr Baxter was subdued. He had already heard from his customers about Polly's impressive feats. There was no longer any talk of selling her. 'Of course, the motor van still has a lot of potential . . .' he said.

'I enjoyed listening to that old man,' said Mark after they had left the café. 'It would be nice to go back to horse-drawn transport in some ways. But I bet we'd miss having cars.'

'We must have seen about a third of the exhibition by now,' said Mo, as they entered another darkened room and were immediately struck by a huge hologram that almost covered the facing wall. It showed an enormous glacier.

Catch Me If I Fall

'I hate my father. How dare he abandon me like this! So much for our holiday together.' Joanna Finch glowered at her expensive monogrammed suitcase, her resentment plain for all to see.

'I'm sure you will like it here in Norway,' said her cousin, Astrid, feeling obliged to be polite. 'Come down when you are ready.'

Ignoring her, Joanna proceeded to unpack her suitcase.

She wondered what her mother was doing, on her annual fortnight at the health farm in Surrey. It was a passing thought; Joanna had never really communicated with her mother. Her father was the centre of her universe, and had been for as long as she could remember.

He was a tall, powerful man, with tremendous presence and a razor-sharp intellect. He ran a string of successful businesses, providing every material comfort for his wife and daughter but despite his very active life he had always been there when Joanna had needed him. Although he could sometimes be dominating, he doted on her, calling her his little princess.

Being an excellent horseman himself he had bought Joanna her first pony when she was four, a mischievous black Shetland called Kipper. At first she had been afraid, and it had taken a lot of persuasion to get her into the saddle. But her father had held on to her with one hand while leading Kipper with the other. She had never forgotten his promise – 'I'll catch you if you fall.'

Over the years her confidence had grown under his expert tuition. Her father bought her the best ponies so she could compete in gymkhanas and shows. Her bedroom wall was covered in red rosettes.

This holiday arrangement was the first time he had let her down. Shortly before they were due to leave for Norway a serious problem had cropped up in one of his companies.

'You'll have to go on alone, Joanna,' he had told her. 'This one is a real crisis. I have to stay in London.'

She had protested, pleaded and sulked to no avail.

'You'll like it in Norway. It's so clean and fresh in the fjords. Your Aunt and Uncle are great people and your cousin Astrid is about your age.' He had kissed her on the cheek. 'I'll join you as soon as I can, princess.'

Joanna's relatives lived in a mountain farm perched on rugged slopes in an isolated spot which she considered primitive. She spent the first night in her room, refusing supper. She was determined to be miserable.

The next morning, however, her resolve to continue her hunger strike crumbled and feeling ravenously hungry she joined the family for a breakfast of stewed fruit, heart-shaped waffles, rye bread and goat cheese.

'I'm glad to see you are eating,' said her Aunt. 'I wouldn't want your father to be worried.'

'He doesn't care about me,' announced Joanna between mouthfuls of cheese. 'And if he phones, I don't want to talk to him.'

'You like horses?' asked Astrid in an attempt to make conversation.

'I might do.'

Astrid was undeterred. 'I have two ponies,' she continued.

Joanna began to look more interested.

'Would you like to ride with me after breakfast?'

Joanna hesitated, not wishing to appear too keen. 'Alright then.'

'Good,' said Astrid and her mother shot her an approving glance. They were anxious that their guest should feel welcome.

Joanna could not hide her disappointment when she saw Astrid's ponies. They were Fjord ponies, muscular and compact with strong short legs. They were both light dun, with a distinctive black dorsal stripe.

'They're not exactly thoroughbreds,' she said scornfully.

Astrid ignored her. 'They are called Freya and Magnus. Freya is the darker of the two.'

'My pony is an Anglo-Arab chestnut called Sahara,' said Joanna.

'These ponies are ideally suited to the terrain around here. They are completely reliable and very tough.' Astrid started to saddle up. 'You can ride Magnus. He is the quieter of the two.'

'I have been riding since I was four years old,' announced Joanna indignantly. 'I can handle any pony.'

'Nevertheless,' continued Astrid. 'You will ride Magnus. Freya does not like strangers.'

Magnus was a steady but self-willed pony and each time Joanna tried to push him ahead into a trot he hung back, reluctant to leave Freya.

'Don't you think it is beautiful here?' asked Astrid.

Joanna could not help agreeing that the scenery was indeed breathtaking but her pride prevented her from voicing this.

The snow covered glacier slopes were hung with tufts of wild flowers and stunning rock formations abounded. The only intrusion on the peace and quiet was the bubbling of the mountain streams.

It was a damp morning and wisps of mist hung between

the rock cliffs. 'Sometimes whole clouds cover the road in white mist,' said Astrid.

They rode on in agreeable silence and Joanna was beginning to get used to Magnus when Astrid said, 'We ought to get back now. I agreed to help mother with lunch.'

'I'll see you later then,' said Joanna.

'What do you mean? You must come back with me. You don't know your way around.'

Joanna looked angry. 'This is supposed to be my holiday. Why should I spoil it because you want to be a killjoy? Anyway, can't your mother cook the meal by herself?'

'You are selfish and spoilt, Joanna. I'm going back now. Are you coming or not? I warn you, if you stay you are liable to get lost.'

'I'm staying out here,' replied Joanna adamantly.

'Well, don't say I didn't warn you. For goodness' sake stay on the track.' She turned Freya and rode away.

Magnus began to follow her and Joanna had great difficulty in persuading him to stay behind. She watched as Astrid wove her way down the zig-zagging mountain slope until she had disappeared from view. The fjords seemed more silent than ever now that Joanna was alone. She pushed Magnus into a reluctant trot. It was colder than she had expected; indeed a wind was starting to gather force.

Magnus ambled along at a leisurely pace, sticking to the narrow road. Joanna was unaware of the sheer drop at the edge to the frozen lake below. Feeling suddenly exhilarated, she wondered how high they could go – perhaps to the top of the mountain. 'Come on, Magnus. This way,' she urged him. But Magnus refused to leave the track and dug his heels in. Joanna kicked his sides and shouted, to no avail. Then she slapped his neck hard with the reins and to her surprise he curved into the air and bucked. Joanna lost her balance and hit the ground hard.

She didn't know for how long she had been unconscious, but when she finally came round she began to panic. She was miles away from the farm, with no idea how to reach it. Her head ached.

Then she thought of her father. If he had not left her alone it would never have happened. She felt betrayed. He had promised always to take care of her, always to be there. He had let her down. Her desperation growing, she looked around her. Just feet away was Magnus, waiting patiently.

She could hardly believe her eyes. Standing up stiffly, Joanna went across to him and mounted. 'Sahara would never have waited,' she said. 'He's a bit temperamental, really. Perhaps too temperamental.'

Magnus made his way along the track, as sure-footed as a mountain goat.

'I hope you know the way, Magnus. I don't.'

Joanna's thoughts were rushing inside her head in a jumble. She felt vulnerable and exposed on the mountain, forced to put all her trust in Magnus. She began to reflect on her life and realized how unhappy she was. It seemed like a blinding revelation but, inside, Joanna had known all along that things were not right.

'Do you know, Magnus, I don't even like riding.' She laughed. 'It sounds so silly. I always wanted to please Daddy. He wants me to be a showjumper. I could do it, too. But if I'm honest with myself, I don't really want to.' Magnus walked on steadily, his ears flicking back and forth like antennae as he listened to the sound of Joanna's voice.

She poured her heart out to the sturdy Fjord pony and before she knew it the farm was in sight. 'You did it, Magnus. You got us home.' She patted his neck. 'I've made a decision. I'm going to tell Daddy that I want to give up riding. Instead, I'm going to be an actress. Of course, he'll be very disappointed.'

Astrid rushed out to meet her. 'Thank goodness. I was about to send out a search party,' she said. 'Here, I'll put Magnus away.'

Joanna did not argue and handed over the reins.

Her Aunt was setting the table. 'Hello, Joanna. Did you have a nice ride, dear?'

'Yes thank you,' replied Joanna, brimming over with her new-found confidence.

'Princess! Haven't you got a kiss for your father?' The voice was warm but insistent.

Joanna turned to see her father standing in the doorway.

His unexpected appearance threw her off guard and she felt her resolve draining. She cleared her throat. 'Daddy, there's something we need to talk about – '

'Not now, Joanna, I want to show you what I bought for you.' He ushered her into the lounge, his firm hand on her shoulder.

Never mind, Joanna told herself weakly. I can tell him later; maybe tonight, or tomorrow, or the next day . . .

'Look at this hologram of a pistol,' said Mark, walking round it. 'It's so real you feel you could pick it up and fire it.' The barrel of the pistol mesmerized the children.

Jack's Ride
(or The Highwayman Repaid)

On Tuesday morning Thomas Neal was executed at Tyburn for robbing the Northern Stage near Highgate.

Morning Chronicle, 23 November 1764.

'Well, Jack, one day it will be your name in the *Chronicle*,' said the elegantly dressed woman, putting down the newspaper.

'Never, Esther. There isn't a rope strong enough that will hang Jack Derby.'

He downed another tankard of ale. 'I must bid you farewell for now. I hear the Duke of Ganerly shortly returns from a pleasant evening at the theatre. I intend to relieve him of his purse.' He roughly pulled Esther to his chest, pressed his lips to hers and quickly took his leave.

With a mask across his face and a brace of pistols at his side, he mounted Nan, his dark bay mare and disappeared into the darkness.

When he had reached the part of the heath across which the Duke's coach must pass he concealed himself under the trees and waited. He smiled, warmed by the touch of his wealthy mistress's lips and excited by the prospect of robbing yet another aristocratic traveller.

The eldest son of a parson, Jack Derby had taken easily to the life of a highwayman when his small grocery had run into debt. He needed a plentiful supply of money to indulge his pleasures; gaming and drinking. As he had anticipated, the Duke's coach soon appeared and Jack rushed out from his cover. Aiming a pistol at the driver's head he shouted to the Duke, 'Out, you poxy dog, lest I cut you to pieces!'

The Duke, accustomed to the perils that Highwaymen presented to men such as himself, hurled his purse from the window of the coach without hesitation. In an instant, Jack had retrieved it from the ground. He was about to demand more when he heard the sound of galloping horses in the distance. He guessed at once that it was the Horse Patrol.

'You'll be hanged, you rogue,' said the Duke as Jack leapt onto Nan's back and made for the woods.

Nan thundered on, stumbling in the deep water-filled ruts and leaping muddy ditches. Jack urged her onwards, using his spurs and whip. He was racing for his very life, the hangman's noose in his mind's eye. As the distance between himself and the Horse Patrol narrowed he became more desperate. Up ahead, a huge five-barred gate loomed, the full moon casting a spectral light upon it.

Nan was tiring, her breath rasping. Jack cast a look over his shoulder at the Horse Patrol. Before he knew it, the gate was before them. 'Over, beast!' he yelled, striking the whip across her flanks.

But it was too late; Nan did not have enough time to clear the gate and she crashed into it, her forelegs hitting it hard. Jack was flung into the air and thrown clear. Bruised and shaking he got to his feet to see the mare stretched out on the grass, her neck broken.

'Damn the mare!' he shouted. The Horse Patrol would catch up with him now, for certain. He ran until he thought his heart would burst, his pursuers closing in.

Just as he was giving up hope he saw smoke coming from a chimney, in a clearing in the woods. Jack knew the terrain like the back of his hand, but he had never before noticed this house. No matter, he thought. The occupants were sure to have a horse. A fresh mount would save his skin.

Not troubling to knock on the door he put his shoulder to it and broke it down.

The room was lit by a single candle and in the shadows Jack could just make out a young woman, seated at the kitchen table.

'I need a horse,' said Jack, raising his pistols.

The woman said nothing.

'Get me a horse, you whore, if you wish to live,' he spat.

The woman stood up slowly.

'How much are you prepared to pay?' she asked, a smile curling her lips.

'Did you not hear, woman? I am Jack Derby, the highwayman. I take what I desire. I pay for nothing.'

'In the stable, then,' the woman replied, still smiling. 'There you will find a horse.' Under her breath she muttered, 'And you will pay.'

Jack ran outside and flung open the stable door. Inside was a magnificent horse, eighteen hands high, the blackest beast Jack had ever set eyes on. The horse was already saddled up, as if it had been waiting for him. He sprang lightly into the saddle and pushed the horse into action.

Horse and rider swept over the desolate heath, the horse's hooves pounding the turf. Jack found he hardly had to use spurs or whip to convince the animal to keep up its speed and gradually he started to edge away from his pursuers, having the advantage of a fresh horse.

Eventually, after an hour, the Horse Patrol gave up the chase and disappeared from sight. Relief swept over Jack.

'Good, my gallant beast, you are a find indeed. No man in England can outrun me if you are my mount.'

Finally, when twenty miles had been put between himself

and the town, Jack decided it would be safe to stop at the next inn. He was in need of sleep and had developed a mighty thirst.

'Whoa, my fine creature,' commanded Jack and he pulled on the reins. But the black horse did not slow his pace. 'Whoa, I said.' Jack's voice changed, the tone hardening. He pulled with all his strength, but the black horse galloped onwards, past the inn and over the heath.

Jack was angry and a little disturbed. No horse had ever outwitted him. His riding skill was renowned throughout the county. But however hard he pulled, the horse galloped on without hindrance or pause. 'He will soon become tired,' Jack told himself.

The hours passed and night turned into day as the dawn broke. Still the black horse showed no signs of fatigue. They passed a gibbet, the iron cage containing the decomposing corpse swinging from side to side in the wind. Jack hardly noticed. Exhausted, he had slumped forward in the saddle, his eyes heavy.

As the day progressed, the skies opened and rain beat down in torrents, quickly soaking horse and rider. Jack thought he must be having a nightmare. The horse could not possibly keep up its pace without bursting its heart. He had given up pulling on the reins, since the horse did not seem to notice any pressure on its mouth.

Suddenly Jack decided to throw himself from the saddle. He was prepared to risk breaking some bones if he could rid himself of this demon horse. But to his disbelief and terror Jack discovered that he was unable to move his legs. It was as if he had been fixed solidly to the saddle.

The day stretched into night and man and horse crossed county after county. Jack realized with chilling certainty that the black horse would never stop.

For Jack Derby had stolen the devil's horse.

Mark led the way to the next picture.

It was of a row of stables under the moonlight, with a midnight blue sky studded by white stars. There was an eerie feel to the picture. Mo looked at it for some time before saying, 'I wonder if there are any horses in the stable?'

The Inheritance

A week before the letter came, Gabrielle had been living in London with her French mother, wondering what to do with herself. They shared a cluttered ground floor flat in Hammersmith, its claustrophobic nature accentuated by the fact that her mother, Suzanne, worked from home as a freelance journalist. 'You are eighteen, Gabby. It's about time you made a decision about your future. You can't mope around the flat forever. Frankly, we are getting on each other's nerves.'

Gabrielle knew her mother was right. She had finished her A levels the previous year and spent the past few months doing a string of jobs, working in bookshops and cafés and becoming increasingly bored.

'Why don't you stay with your father for a while?' her mother suggested. Gabrielle shrugged.

'Dad has a new girlfriend. I don't think they will want me hanging around.'

Gabrielle's parents had been divorced for five years and her English father, who was an actor, lived in Sussex. It had been an amicable arrangement, and both parents were the best of friends.

'Why not do a secretarial course, Gabby?' her mother said. 'Being bilingual will be a big advantage.'

'But I don't want to be a secretary,' moaned Gabrielle.

'You don't have to stay a secretary. It's the way to get on. Everyone knows that. That's how I got my job.'

'So you keep telling me.' Gabrielle took an apple from

the fruit bowl and wandered over to the window. She did not relish going out to work at all. However, some extra money would not come amiss.

'All right. I'll go and register for a typing course on Monday. Satisfied?'

Her mother smiled. 'Whatever you want, cherie.'

When she returned from the secretarial agency on Monday morning she found her mother holding the letter.

'It's from a solicitor. My father has been killed in an accident'.

Gabrielle could not think of anything to say.

'He and I never got on. We haven't been in contact for many years. To be honest, Gabrielle, we did not like each other much.' She looked at her daughter. 'You, however, are a different matter.'

'What do you mean?'

'He has left you his chateau in Brittany.'

Gabrielle's mouth dropped open. 'You must be joking.'

'No joke, Gabby. It's all yours. Every gloomy inch of it. On the condition that you live there. So what will you do?'

This is the answer to my prayers, thought Gabrielle. I am so bored here. Living in France, in an old chateau . . . A shiver went down her spine as she thrilled to the idea. What an adventure! She stood up and faced her mother. 'I will keep it,' she announced. 'I will go and live there. How soon before I can leave?'

The sea crossing to Brittany had been uneventful but on arrival at Roscoff, Gabrielle was struck by the landscape of the northern Finistère. A car had been waiting for her at the docks. Now they had left the town and were heading into the countryside. It was Spring, and the hedges were white with hawthorn. It was the most isolated part of Brittany, with Roscoff on the tip of the headland, once a smugglers' stronghold. They passed a watchtower close to the port and drove on to the south side of the town, by an ancient Capuchin convent, followed by a number of chapels and churches. They travelled through St Pol-de-Léon and took the road westwards, following the coast.

'How much further?' Gabrielle asked the driver.

'Nearly there, Mademoiselle,' he replied.

Gabrielle leaned back on the leather seat, enjoying the smooth ride in the big Citroën.

Soon they reached the sheltered resort of Brignogan.

'Beyond here is the coast of legends, the wildest corner of Brittany,' the driver informed her. 'In the past there were many shipwrecks on her perilous reefs. L'Ankou – Death – is never far away from the legends, haunting the night in search of souls,' he said darkly.

But Gabrielle hardly heard his words, so taken was she with the imposing chateau that loomed up ahead on the edge of the cliff. Its grey stone walls and round towers filled her with awe. This feeling became greater still when a host of servants greeted her at the door.

Her room was in the east tower, up three flights of stairs and filled with ornately carved furniture, including a chaise longue and a four poster bed. As she was feeling tired, an evening meal of seafood crêpes and a goblet of fine muscadet were brought to her room. Before retiring, she stood at the huge window watching the sunset. Her eye soon fell on the stables below. She counted ten loose boxes.

'My dream will be complete if those stables are full of horses,' she murmured. A shrill whinny cutting through the evening dusk answered her prayer.

After a breakfast of croissants and coffee, again served in her room, Gabrielle set off for the stables.

The door of the first loose box was open and a dappled grey horse was inside, tethered to an iron ring in the wall.

He was resting a hindleg, looking bored. Gabrielle whistled and the horse pricked his ears and turned his head.

'He is called Louis. He is handsome, eh?'

The husky voice at Gabrielle's shoulder made her jump. He introduced himself. 'I am Léon, the Head Groom. Do you ride, Mademoiselle Kirby?'

'When I can afford it,' she replied.

'Now, it seems, money will not prevent you from doing so. You have nine horses to choose from.'

Gabrielle laughed. 'You're right. I hadn't thought of it like that. I am still getting used to this new life.'

'Let me show you your other horses,' said Léon.

There was Triphine, another dappled grey and the sister of Louis; Dahut, a tall bay mare with a Roman nose; Étoile, a silver thoroughbred; Salome, a strawberry roan mare, who Gabrielle was warned had a tendency to bite; a pair of Carmargue horses, Tristan and Iseult, and Marguerite, a clipped chestnut hunter.

'They are all beautiful,' commented Gabrielle. 'But I thought you said there were nine horses. I have only counted eight.'

Léon gestured towards the loose box at the end of the stable block. 'You should not approach this horse,' he warned. 'It is the stallion, Malo.'

'Why not?' asked Gabrielle.

'This horse killed your grandfather. Malo kicked him to death in that stable.'

'Good heavens,' gasped Gabrielle. 'But why has he not been destroyed, if he is dangerous?'

'He was your grandfather's favourite horse. It was in his will that you should inherit all the horses. Including Malo.'

'I would be curious to see this horse,' said Gabrielle.

'I will show you, then. You can look – but do not touch.'

Gabrielle felt a strange thrill when she saw Malo. He

was an intense blue-black, with flashing eyes. His Spanish blood was evident in his high arched crest and sweeping curly mane and tail. Léon cursed the horse in French and Malo laid his ears back and glared at them.

Gabrielle was fascinated by the horse and seized with a desire to ride him. When Léon turned to walk away she lingered, admiring the horse's magnificent conformation.

'I know what you are thinking,' said Léon. 'Put the thought from your mind. It is every young girl's fantasy to tame the untameable. You will be killed if you try.'

Gabrielle fumed at being spoken to as if she were a silly schoolgirl. Smarting from her wounded pride, she became more determined to prove Léon wrong. On her way back to the house she encountered Alain, one of the stable lads.

'Bonjour,' he said in a friendly voice. 'You must be Gabrielle.'

She returned his smile. Alain was in his late twenties, with warm eyes and sun-bleached hair.

'I would like to ride this morning,' she said. 'Which horse would you recommend? I am spoilt for choice!'

'Who would you like to ride?' asked Alain.

'Malo.'

He shook his head. 'Salome, she is the most reliable and quiet ride.'

'Léon told me she bites.'

'In the stable, perhaps, she can be bad tempered. But when she is ridden, she is a perfect lady.' He laughed. 'She is a little eccentric. But she is old. We can allow old people their eccentricities.'

This prompted Gabrielle's next question: 'What was grandfather like? Was he an eccentric?'

'Perhaps. He was grief stricken when his ill-health prevented him from riding. He lived for horses. It was ironic how he died.'

They rode down to the beach, with Alain on Dahut, who was in high spirits, sidestepping and swishing her tail. As Alain had promised, Salome was a comfortable and reassuring mount and knew the route well enough to need little instruction from her rider. Gabrielle reflected on how wonderful it was to be in the saddle again.

'Grandfather must have been very rich to afford all this,' she commented. Alain grinned.

'He managed. He had a great many investments; enough to keep the chateau running for some years to come. Then, when the money runs out, you will have to make the decisions about what to do with it all.'

'I never really knew Grandfather. I was only four when I last saw him. He and mother were always arguing. In that huge portrait of him at the top of the stairs he looks like such a gentle man.'

The time seemed to pass quickly before Alain said, 'I must get back now. I have plenty of work to do. But you stay. Enjoy yourself. Salome will take care of you.'

'Thank you, Alain. Before you go, may I ask one last question?'

'Of course. What do you want to know?'

'How did it happen, Alain? How could grandfather have suffered such an accident?'

'I still find it hard to believe myself,' he replied.

'Is there any doubt, then, that it was an accident?' she persisted.

There was a long silence before Alain replied: 'He was kicked to death. There is no question about that. The mystery is why?'

'Léon says Malo is dangerous. Why should Grandfather keep such a horse? It puzzles me.'

'Let me tell you something about Malo. Your grandfather rescued him. The horse was found tethered in a deserted barn on a short rope. He had been left to starve.'

'Oh, that is dreadful.'

'That is not all,' continued Alain. 'While he was tethered and unable to escape, Malo was attacked by rats. His legs were badly bitten.'

'How bizarre. Poor Malo.'

'Because of this, Malo became very neurotic. If anything gets under his feet, he goes berserk. I dropped a brush once, when I was grooming him. He trampled it into the straw and it was hours before he would calm down.'

'Was he broken in when you got him? Had he ever been ridden?'

'We don't know. It was your grandfather's dream to ride him. But he became ill, so it never happened. Your grandfather loved that horse and Malo did show affection to him. This is why what happened is such a mystery.'

With that, Alain turned Dahut towards the chateau.

The next morning, Gabrielle visited Malo. Since the accident he had been shunned by everyone and she was determined to win his confidence. She chatted to him for hours, telling him all about her life in England and her journey to France. At first, he ignored her, preferring to stand, almost cowering, in a safe corner of his stable. But gradually he moved nearer to her until he was inches away. Her heart began to beat faster as he stretched out his nose to smell her.

'Get away from that horse!' a voice shouted, making Gabrielle nearly jump out of her skin.

It was Léon. 'I warned you. You'll get hurt.'

'You idiot.' Gabrielle turned on him. 'I was just winning his trust. Now you've ruined everything. You've scared him off.'

'It is you, arrogant child, who are the idiot,' retorted

Léon. 'Anyway, I came to tell you that you have a phone call. It is your mother.'

Gabrielle stormed back to the house.

She decided to continue her taming of Malo at dusk when it was quiet and she would be alone.

The moon shed an eerie light across the yard and an unaccountable foreboding crept up on her. Malo was standing in the corner of his stable and this time she decided to go in with him. At first, he laid back his ears and Gabrielle, murmuring reassurances to him, wondered if she was doing the right thing. But slowly both she and Malo began to relax.

It was approaching midnight when the breakthrough came. Finally, Malo came over to her and she was able to stroke his nose. He whinnied softly and Gabrielle felt tears in her eyes as the horse that had been labelled a killer nuzzled against her.

Suddenly she felt a sharp pain on the back of her head and she slumped on to the straw. Malo squealed and she was aware of shouting, and pain in her leg as the horse kicked out. The next thing she knew, Malo was towering above her, his sharp hooves inches away. As she lost consciousness she heard an earth shattering bang . . .

'I think she's coming round now,' a woman's voice murmured. 'Are you feeling better, Gabrielle?'

Gabrielle opened her eyes to see the housekeeper standing over her.

'You're safe in bed now, cherie. There was an accident.'

Gabrielle's head ached.

'What happened? I can't remember.'

'That dreadful horse tried to kick you to death, just like your grandfather. Whatever were you doing in the stable?'

'I . . . I was trying to –'

'Well, you needn't worry, that horse won't hurt anyone again.'

'What do you mean?' Gabrielle asked fearfully.

'Léon shot him. Lucky he found you. He saved your life.'

It was several days before the doctor would allow Gabrielle out of bed. There was a long cut on her leg where Malo had kicked her and she had suffered from concussion. She felt sick and listless, trying to remember what had happened and was desperately sad about Malo.

When she got up her leg was sore but she went down to the stables. Alain looked pleased to see her. 'We were all worried. How are you feeling?'

'Fine,' she replied, looking in the direction of Malo's stable. 'I can't believe he's gone. He was so beautiful.' Alain said nothing.

'I wish I could ride but the doctor has forbidden it. He says my leg is still weak.'

'If you really want to, we could go out on the two Carmargues. They are trained to neck rein and respond to voice commands.'

Gabrielle's face lit up. 'I would love to.'

Alain tacked up Tristan and Iseult and they set off across her grandfather's estate.

'What will you do now, Gabrielle?' Alain asked her.

'What do you mean?'

'We wondered if you would leave now, after what has happened.'

'If I leave, I will lose the chateau and the horses. It was a condition of the will. If I go, the estate would revert to Léon.'

She was thoughtful for a while.

'What would happen to the estate if Léon took over?'

'He would probably try and sell the chateau to property developers and get rid of the horses.'

'But why?'

Alain laughed. 'Money, of course. He claims that the estate is on a landslide and the property will eventually be worthless, so he needs to sell as soon as possible. If you ask me, he's making it up; just an excuse to cover up his greed. It was a bit of a shock to him when you turned up here.'

Gabrielle turned this over in her mind.

'Alain, who found Grandfather after the accident?'

'Léon.'

'Who found me?'

'Léon.'

'And my accident was the same as Grandfather's?'

'Gabrielle, what are you saying? Léon saved your life. If he hadn't been there – '

'But why was he there?' asked Gabrielle. 'It was midnight.'

'He said he heard a noise and went to investigate. When he got there you were lying in the straw and Malo was attacking you.'

'The doctor said I must have fallen down after Malo kicked me and then hit my head on the floor. But I fell down *before* Malo kicked me. It was as if something had hit me on the head. Or someone.'

Gabrielle slept uneasily that night. If her theory was right, then it meant that Léon was a murderer. He had knocked her grandfather down into the straw, knowing that Malo went crazy if anything, particularly anything moving, was under his feet. He probably watched the old man being kicked to death. And he had planned a similar accident for her, stopping short of seeing her killed, making himself look the hero, with the hope of scaring her into giving up the property and returning to England. She shivered. His plan had not succeeded. Would he try again?

Poor Malo had just been a pawn in his plan. The beautiful horse had been used and destroyed.

For the rest of the week Gabrielle avoided Léon, instead channelling her energies into schooling the thoroughbred Étoile. He was young and green and Alain was convinced he had the makings of a racer.

She had still not decided whether to stay at the chateau or return to England. 'Self-preservation,' she told herself, 'should be your priority.' But another part of her refused to give in, determined to stay in the chateau that now belonged to her. The feeling was reinforced whenever she passed Malo's empty stable. If Léon really had arranged the 'accidents' then Malo was not to blame. But she could never prove it.

At night she sometimes imagined that she heard Malo pacing his stables and whinnying and she remembered how on the night of his death he had shown her affection.

The other horses seemed more easily spooked since then and a strange atmosphere seemed to pervade the stables. She was certain that Alain had also noticed this but he said nothing.

Gabrielle became irritable and on edge, expecting Léon to arrange some other mishap for her. It was a question of where and when.

Exactly one week after Malo's death she was awoken in the night by noises coming from the stables. She went over to the window. She could make out a shadow by Malo's stable and she pulled on a coat to investigate. It was foggy and as she breathed in the damp air she wondered if Léon had engineered the situation, and was luring her outside. She opened the stable door and cautiously peered inside.

What she saw rooted her to the spot.

Léon was pushed against the wall, his arms spread wide, his face ashen white. His features were distorted with terror and before her eyes his hair seemed to turn grey. He turned his head towards her, his breathing harsh. 'Help me,' he pleaded, his voice barely audible.

'What is it?' she cried. 'What are you afraid of?' She followed his frozen gaze and in an instant she knew. She heard the sound of hooves crashing on the stone floor and for a second saw glowing, demonic eyes through the darkness.

Suddenly Alain had joined her, flashing his torch into the darkness. 'What in God's name is going on?'

The torch revealed Léon huddled in the corner of an empty stable.

'Malo is here,' Léon blurted. He stared at Gabrielle and the look they exchanged confirmed her suspicions about his part in the accidents.

'Tell them,' he begged. 'You saw him. He was here.'

'What does he mean?' asked Alain, bewildered.

Gabrielle's eyes never left Léon's. 'I don't know what he's talking about,' she said. 'The man is obviously going mad.'

Léon left the chateau at the crack of dawn in a great hurry.

Walking across the stable yard later that morning the air smelt fresh and clean and Gabrielle felt glad to be alive.

She saddled Triphine and set off for the beach, making plans for the future. They rode through the sea and galloped along the sand before stopping for Gabrielle to gaze with pride upon the chateau on the cliff, secure in the knowledge that Léon could not take it away.

She returned home in triumph, unaware of the slow but inexorable crumbling of the earth and rock beneath the chateau.

Mo turned towards the next exhibit and almost jumped out of her skin.

'Good heavens! I thought it was a real person!'

Inches from her face was a life-size hologram of a man from the past.

'He looks a bit like a cowboy,' commented Mark, 'and so real.'

'He must be a working model, because his lips are moving,' said Mo.

It was as if the figure was speaking to them . . .

The Hardest Ride

I had loved horses all my life and remembered well my first pony, Darlington, a plucky bay mare. So naturally I applied for a job with the Pony Express, and was accepted.

I was used to being in the saddle all day and I thought I was tough enough to ride for the Pony Express. I had been told that the work was hard and dangerous, and as I approached the corral I began to feel apprehensive.

There were six horses in the corral; small, wiry mustangs that had been taught to stay on the trail no matter what happened. I had heard tales of riders falling from the saddle exhausted, and of a rider shot by Indians, but their horses still bringing the mail pouch safely to the next station on time.

I was handed a dun pony called Haydn and a mailbag was fastened to the saddle.

'You ride four stages today. But remember to change horses each time,' said the boss. He slapped Haydn's rump and we were away.

Fifteen miles of rugged country had to be covered before we would reach the next station. My horse had a long steady stride and stretched his neck eagerly. At last the station appeared and I pulled up Haydn, patted his neck quickly and vaulted on to the horse that was being held for me. In a matter of two minutes the mail pouch was transferred to my new mount, a sorrel stallion called Russet, and soon we were racing to cover another fifteen miles. Open country stretched ahead. The pure exhilaration of speed drugged my mind as I urged Russet faster and faster until we were hurtling along at a breakneck pace. Then Russet stumbled and suddenly we were somersaulting through the air, and I met the ground with a resounding thud.

When I recovered I expected to see Russet galloping into the distance as he had been trained to do. But when I looked round he was standing there, head hanging, reins broken. I walked towards him and spoke soothingly. A deep cut stretched from his knee to cannon bone. I tore off a strip of my shirt and bound the wound tightly. I led Russet up and down for a few minutes but he didn't seem too lame so I knotted the reins and mounted. I remembered the rules; 'Mail first, horse second, rider last' and realized the mail was late. But now I didn't care and my main concern was for the horse.

As I rode away I felt a trickle of blood on my forehead. I hastily wiped it away and looked down to see the offending stone streaked red with my blood. Sluggishly, I nudged Russet's sides and we continued to the next station. As I approached, I blew the horn to indicate my approach. Russet would be glad of a rest, I thought. A man stood by the empty corral holding a grey horse. I halted Russet and threw my reins to the man.

'Quick, the mail bag!' I yelled.

'But she's lame,' the man protested as I mounted the grey horse.

'Well, aren't there any more horses here?' I asked.

'No, they were all used to chase bandits who stole some mail. There's only Sonnet here left, but she's lame. I'm sorry but you'll have to continue on your red horse.'

I hesitated, then mounted Russet again. 'Come on fella, you can rest at the next station,' I told him sighing. The ride was proving demanding and each stride Russet took seemed harder than the last. My head ached now and I longed for a bed.

Then I heard them.

Whistling arrows and blood-curdling shrieks cut through the air.

I remembered my instructions; then I thought of Russet. How could I possibly ask him to go any faster? The shouts of the dangerously close Indians persuaded me. I raised the strap and lashed it against my boot. The crack startled Russet and his ears lay flat against his neck as he galloped like a mad beast, attempting to outrun the Indians. I thought his heart would burst. The ear-splitting sound of the Indians seemed nearer every second and my legs flailed against Russet's foam-flecked sides as I yelled at him, willing him to go faster. He was blowing like crazy, his neck caked in sweat. I thought for sure he would be broken-winded by the time we reached the next station – if we reached it.

The wind whistled past my ears and gradually the sound of the Indians grew fainter as they gave up the chase. Russet stumbled over rocks and boulders, cutting and bruising his legs. I was glad when we had to ford through a river for the water cooled his legs and soothed his wounds. Eventually we reached the station and, exhausted, I fell from Russet's saddle as he halted.

But when I climbed out of the dust and looked around something told me the place was deserted. As I searched the station a terrible feeling of desperation swept over me. I dragged myself outside again and looked in the corral. It was empty. I knew reluctantly what I had to do.

'I'm sorry, Russet,' I told him.

I swung my leg over the saddle and we loped away from the station. The dried blood on my forehead irritated and I felt completely drained of strength. Russet galloped on bravely. His bandage was soaked red but his leg had stopped bleeding.

Suddenly a knawing blackness clouded my mind and I slumped over Russet's shoulder, my hand tangled in the reins. God knows how I stayed on, but eventually I reached the station on my faithful mount.

The next thing I knew I was lying in a bed with a clean bandage around my head. Bill Travers, the foreman, was standing over me.

'How are you feeling, Jack?' he asked.

I groaned. 'How do you think?'

'Don't worry, the mail has been taken to the next station by the relief rider,' Bill said.

'What about Russet?' I asked. 'How is he?'

Bill hesitated. 'His legs are a bit of a mess and they will be scarred permanently. It's a wonder he didn't collapse. He's an exceptional horse. But the vet's looked at him and he thinks he'll probably pull through,' He smiled. 'He's a tough little feller. He'll soon be ready to carry the mail again.'

I got to my feet. 'I'd like to see him.'

Russet was in his stall and he lifted his head and whickered when he saw me. Bill looked surprised. 'That's the first time he's responded to anybody. He must have taken to you.'

'I sure have taken to him,' I replied, fussing over the horse. 'What happened at the last station?'

'It seems someone let the horses loose and the men had to catch them again,' Bill told me.

After thinking for a few minutes I said, 'I'm going to buy Russet.'

Bill gasped, 'But . . .'

'Look, Bill, I know he was one of the best horses, but he's young. It wouldn't be fair to make him gallop that distance every day under these conditions; it would be too cruel. If I bought him he'd have a life worth living. He'd make a good ranch horse and he could probably be used for chuck-wagon racing. He's very suited to it and he loves to gallop. I'll discuss it with the boss.'

Fourteen months later the Pony Express was replaced by the railroad. But in the eighteen months it was in action the Pony Express came to symbolize speed, courage and stamina of horse and rider.

'Look, Mark, these are those kind of holograms that you can buy in the shops.'

Mark followed her gaze. Assembled on a high table were three small transparent blocks, each seeming to contain a different object. In the first was a ring of matted grey hair; in the second a pink feather plume. The third contained a pencil.

Mo picked one up and rotated it. 'I bet each one has a story to tell.'

The Cure

The grey mare winced in pain as the vet finished his examination.

'It's as I thought, Martin. She has an arthritic back. It can only get worse.' The colour drained from the boy's face as the vet's pronouncement sank in. 'Being ridden causes her great pain. The fairest thing would be to have her put down.'

Supper that night was a silent affair as Martin relived his past year with the speckled Connemara mare he called Ophelia.

He had bought her at an auction, attracted by her striking looks and lively temperament. Boy and pony had quickly developed an attachment, becoming inseparable.

Her impressive jumping ability had scooped up a collection of red rosettes and trophies. Martin felt guilty that he hadn't noticed her affliction earlier. When she had started to refuse to jump he had blamed his own riding ability, although he had wondered if she was off-colour. But soon she became stiff and reluctant to canter. When she refused to be saddled the vet had been called.

'You mustn't blame yourself, Martin,' his mother told him.

'I feel so guilty, causing her pain by continuing to ride her,' he replied.

'It's too late for recriminations,' said his father. 'The vet is right – if she won't improve we should let him put her out of her misery.'

Martin bit his lip to stop the tears. 'I know. I just wanted time to say goodbye.'

'The vet is not coming back until Monday. At least that gives you a couple of days . . .' His mother's voice trailed off.

'Look, Martin, we know how hard this is for you,' his father said. 'Why don't you come with me to Cornwall on Sunday night. The break will do you good. That way, you won't be here when the vet is – ' He stopped abruptly.

'Your father is right. It would make a nice change. You can stay away for a few days. It won't hurt to miss school once in a while.'

'The countryside is beautiful,' agreed his father. 'While I'm finalizing arrangements with the gallery for my latest exhibition you can wander where you like. When we come back, you can look for a new pony.'

Martin rushed from the table, knocking his chair over. 'I don't want another pony!' he shouted. 'I want Ophelia.'

Cornwall held few charms for Martin as he stared from the window of the guest house on Sunday night. He thought about his farewell to Ophelia before he had left, how she had nuzzled in his pockets for the polo mints he always carried. In her customary manner she had crunched them loudly, slobbering over his shoulder, her eyes trusting and loving.

Martin swallowed hard, overwhelmed with the feeling that he had betrayed her. 'Damn it!' he snapped at the empty room.

Unable to cope with the silence, he switched on the radio at full volume. Anything was preferable to these morbid thoughts, even late night politics on the radio.

Martin couldn't sleep, and finally, in the early hours of the morning, he got up and dressed.

A sick feeling hit him when he realized it was already Monday. Although it was raining outside, he set off for a walk across country.

The rain soaked through his jumper and plastered his mousey hair to his forehead. He had been walking for twenty minutes when he heard a strange high-pitched sound, like a baby crying. Searching in the undergrowth he discovered a very young siamese cat, soaking wet and highly distressed. His paw was caught in a poacher's snare, the wire cutting deep.

'Poor creature.' Martin bent down and the cat pulled away. 'Keep still,' he told it, trying to release the injured paw.

By the time he had finished, his hand was badly scratched and the cat was exhausted. He took off his sweater and wrapped it around the cat and carried the bundle in his arms.

'We need to get you some help.' He scanned the landscape. There was only one building for miles around and he headed for that.

The house looked dilapidated and the garden was so overgrown it threatened to take over. Walking up the weedstrewn path Martin felt sure no one could live there.

The door was open and he peered inside. The walls were bare plaster and exposed brickwork. In the corner of the room was a low table, covered with pots and empty jars, a collection of assorted teapots and a loaf of stale bread. Huge bundles of dried herbs and flowers hung from beams in the ceiling and a sweet scent pervaded the air.

A girl appeared as if from nowhere and scooped the cat from Martin. 'Persia, my baby, where have you been?'

She was petite, with long auburn hair in a tidy plait and

beautiful green cat-like eyes. She was dressed in a short black dress and an unusual medallion hung from the high neck. Her immaculate appearance seemed incongruous in the shabby surroundings.

'I found him in a snare. He needs a vet,' said Martin.

The girl smiled. 'No need. I can take care of it.' She noticed the scratches on Martin's hand. 'Sit down. I've got some ointment for that.'

Martin hesitated, uncertain of the stranger. The girl laughed. 'I don't bite. Sit down.' She painted the cuts with a clear sticky liquid that smelt of aniseed.

'Thank you for rescuing Persia,' she said. He noticed she was in her late teens, not much older than himself.

'I'll make you some tea. It's the least I can do.'

Martin expected her to brew up tea made from an unusual herb and was surprised, almost disappointed to see her open a box of ordinary teabags. But he was grateful for the refreshment and suddenly realized how cold and wet he was.

He looked at his watch. It was nearly eight-thirty. The vet would soon be on his way to Ophelia.

'You look sad, Martin. What's troubling you?' the girl asked.

'How did you know my name? I never told you,' said Martin nervously, convinced there was something odd about her.

'No mystery. There's a label sewn in your sweater with your name on it.' She handed him back his soggy jumper, covered with cat hairs and blood.

'Now, what's wrong?' she persisted and Martin found himself telling her about Ophelia.

'I know how you must be feeling,' she consoled. 'I think the world of my cat, Persia. It is terrible to lose a friend.'

She touched his hand. 'Ophelia must be a lovely pony. I wish I was able to see her.'

Martin reached into his pocket and produced a thick lock of grey hair tied with red cotton. 'It's from Ophelia's mane. To remember her.'

They continued to talk until Martin finally said, 'I'd better go now. Dad will wonder where I am.' He felt reluctant to leave; the girl was easy to relate to and he felt peaceful in her house.

'Take care, Martin,' she said.

By the time he reached the guest house it was nearly ten o'clock and the cold feeling returned when he thought of the empty paddock. He went to his room and changed into dry clothes. He was rubbing his hair with a towel when there was a knock on the door.

His father entered. 'Your mother has just phoned. Something has happened to Ophelia.'

'What is it, Dad?'

'When the vet arrived she was galloping round the paddock like a yearling. He couldn't believe it. So he examined her again.'

'She's cured?'

His father nodded. 'It's a miracle.'

Martin suddenly felt delirious with joy.

It was on the journey home that he discovered the lock of Ophelia's hair was missing from his pocket and he realized he must have left it at the girl's house.

Circus

Jaf had lost count of the number of times he had witnessed the build-up of the Big Top and watched the flags and banners fluttering in the breeze. Jaf was an Appaloosa gelding, born in a circus in Denmark nineteen years earlier. He was an attractive animal, his distinctive chocolate-spotted coat and mottled pink nose and lips marking him out from all his companions.

He had been brought up in the circus, growing accustomed to the busy routine and the constant travelling throughout the world. He had been trained as a High School horse, and his act included all the basic dressage movements like the passage and piaffe. The highlight of his act was the dance he performed to the tune of *Puppet on a String*. To the audience it appeared that the horse had developed a musical ability and was indeed dancing, when in fact it was the circus band that kept in time with Jaf's movements, accentuating the rhythm of his actions. But lately Jaf had noticed that he was not as fit and supple as he used to be.

He yawned. The morning was the best part of the day. He listened to the sounds of the other animals waking; the elephants trumpeting at their keepers and the lions and tigers roaring. He scraped his hoof along the floor, impatient for breakfast.

He looked across at his companions, who were also anticipating breakfast. Tarik and Mishka, two of the perfectly matched Arab Liberty horses were nuzzling each other and nickering. They were both smokey grey, with dish faces and soft olive eyes with long lashes.

In the next stall was Java, the apricot-coloured mare used for bareback riding. Like all rosinbacks she was an intelligent and supple creature with a broad back, trained to canter slowly and steadily around the ring without breaking step while acrobats leapt on and off her back performing somersaults.

Next to Java was the albino Rani, the other rosinback, who was often paired with Java. He pawed the straw and tossed his head. He was young and prone to bouts of temperament, which on occasion had spoilt the act. Jaf had overheard his groom saying that they may have to get rid of Rani if his behaviour did not improve.

'Grub up.' Jaf's groom, Tony, poured a mixture of oats and bran into the manger and refilled the haynet. 'Let's hope we get a good audience tonight.'

After breakfast Jaf and the other horses were taken out for exercise in the nearby park. For the next few months the circus would stay in England, visiting seaside resorts. This site was outside Brighton so they were expecting a large audience.

When they returned from exercise Jaf was taken into the ring to rehearse, although he knew his act inside out. His rider, Stella, was a slim blonde girl, with an attractive face. She was gentle but firm with Jaf and never lost her temper, which was a contrast to his previous rider, a fierce American lady who had been sacked by the circus owner.

The first performance was in the late afternoon and Jaf was returned to the stable to be groomed and prepared.

The performance went without a hitch, as it always did, with Stella resplendent and glamorous in a glittering costume and tinsel in her hair, while Jaf wore a tall pink plume on his head. The audience cheered and clapped and Jaf left the ring feeling pleased with himself.

The crowd was bigger and noisier for the evening performance but Jaf had been trained not to be spooked by crowds and performed his act with polish and precision. Stella looked elegant riding side-saddle and acknowledged the applause with a charming smile. One of the clowns said, 'Well done,' but Stella shook her head.

'The sparkle has gone.'

The next few days went on as usual, with the exception that Rani was withdrawn from the act with Java and sold. He had ruined an evening performance by throwing his rider and colliding into Java, bruising her shoulder.

Shortly after Rani's departure a horsebox drew up and a magnificent white Andalucian stallion stepped out. He carried his head high and had a showy action. Stella met him and introduced him to his new surroundings. He was to occupy Rani's old stall.

Jaf soon learned that the newcomer was called Regal and had been bought for a considerable sum from a local stud farm. Regal missed his old home and in his initial week at the circus he was restless and irritable. Stella spent a great deal of time with Regal, causing Jaf to feel jealous.

One morning, when Jaf was fidgetting in his stall, waiting for Stella to take him out, Jaf got an unpleasant surprise. Stella entered, looking spruce and cheerful as usual. But instead of coming to see Jaf she went straight past his stall, ignoring him, and saddled up Regal.

Jaf began to feel unsettled. To make matters worse, this pattern continued for the rest of the week and when all the other horses went out to exercise, Jaf was left alone.

On Sunday night at dusk Tony came in to the stable and said to Jaf, 'Time to go, old thing.'

The evening performance was over and Jaf could sense

that all around him people were rushing round to pull down the Big Top. They usually travelled overnight to the next site and Jaf was used to this.

When he was led out to the waiting truck Jaf went without qualms, although the vehicle was not familiar to him. He listened to the sounds of the other animals as he was driven away, recognizing Java's shrill squeal as she reprimanded Mishka for stealing her hay.

The journey lasted barely forty minutes. When the door was opened Jaf stood stock still, taking in the unfamiliar sights and sounds. He looked around for Tony, who was always there when they arrived at a new site. Instead, he was met by a freckled, wiry, boy dressed in a T-shirt and jeans. He took the halter rope and led Jaf into a loose box piled high with sweet smelling straw.

'Welcome to your new home,' the boy said, rubbing Jaf's nose.

When he had explored his new surroundings and nibbled at some hay Jaf thrust his head over the open door. He saw a row of twenty loose boxes, their occupants ranging from retired carthorses to injured thoroughbreds; from once-mistreated ponies to elderly seaside donkeys.

The boy had worked at the horse refuge for nearly a year, lavishing care and attention on all his charges. But he soon developed a particular affection for the Appaloosa circus horse.

Over the years, Jaf continued to age with grace, enjoying his retirement. But whenever a particular tune was played on the radio, the horse's ears would prick up and he would perform his old High School routine to music.

The Horse Sale

'This is the first time I've been to a horse sale,' said Marilyn, her eyes dancing with excitement.

'Me too,' I replied.

We did everything together, me and Marilyn, and had done for as long as I could remember. We had been what you might call 'best friends' since we were toddlers, being next door neighbours. We had gone to the same schools, been in the same classes, sat together, played together, been shopping together – even our birthdays were only two days apart. We swapped clothes, books, and make-up, shared our joys and our problems; we were like sisters.

We were in our early teens when we first became interested in horses and decided to take riding lessons at the local riding school. Neither of us had enough pocket money to ride every week so we would work for rides, which was fine at first, only it was Marilyn who seemed to get the rides while I did the work! It was luck really, but as a result Marilyn progressed quicker and was the better rider of the two of us, which needled me. Recently she had been offered the chance to exercise a horse belonging to a local farmer, whenever she liked. The horse was a cobby skewbald called Dalby and not an easy ride, which was why Marilyn exercised him and not the farmer. Of course, she shared him with me to some extent but he was really 'her' horse. Whenever I told her how lucky she was she protested that he kept bolting with her and really wasn't much fun but I knew she was saying it to stop me feeling envious.

When the farmer eventually sold Dalby I have to admit to feeling secretly pleased; now we were even again.

However, our parents decided shortly after this that they could finally afford to buy us a pony each, the reason being that both my father and Marilyn's worked for the same firm and had recently been given a generous pay rise. Despite our desire to rush out immediately and buy the first horses we saw we decided to be cautious and sensible and look around before committing ourselves. I had known of friends who were able to buy very nice horses for quite low prices at auction, so, despite our lack of expertise, we had set off to see for ourselves.

'The horses and ponies are in Ring 1,' said Marilyn, studying her catalogue.

'The sale doesn't start until noon so we've got an hour to wait. Shall we get something to eat? I'm starving.'

We queued up outside a dingy-looking caravan and bought hotdogs and then wandered into Ring 2 to look at the secondhand riding clothes. Some of them looked in pretty poor condition but there were bargains to be had. I bought myself a pair of navy stretch jodhpurs that looked as if they had never been worn and Marilyn found herself a slightly worn, but serviceable, hacking jacket.

Pleased with our purchases we sauntered into the market to look at the horses waiting in the stalls. A number was tied to the rails of each enclosure and all the animals had a number stuck on them. Three New Forest foals were huddled together in a pen, frightened by the thronging crowds and the sound of the rain drumming on the roof.

'Poor things. It seems so undignified,' I said sadly.

'I would never let my horse be sold at a place like this,' commented Marilyn. We wandered around together, listening to people talking, hoping to pick up some useful information. All the horses looked beautiful to us and we found it hard to decide which ones to consider bidding for. I had picked out three that I was particularly keen on and Marilyn had seen four.

We were on our way back into the ring when we passed Lot 40 and both stopped in our tracks.

In the pen was a strikingly handsome animal, bright chestnut with a light flaxen mane and tail and large brown eyes. He tossed his head at us and pawed the ground, impatient to be out and moving, bored with the standing still all morning.

'He's gorgeous,' we murmured in unison.

'What does it say in the catalogue?' asked Marilyn, thumbing through the pages hurriedly.

'Here we are,' I said. 'Lot 40: HEART OF FIRE, chestnut gelding. 6 years. 15.2 h.h. Forward going. Snaffle mouth. Showing plenty of promise. 100% in all respects. Would suit keen teenager. For sale as owner overstocked.'

'He's for me,' announced Marilyn.

'Hang on, I saw him first,' I argued.

'Don't be silly. We both saw him together. Anyway, it doesn't matter. We're only here for fun, aren't we? I mean, we're not actually going to buy anything?' She laughed uneasily and I laughed too, but there had been an edge to her voice and I was relieved when the auctioneer commanded everyone to take their places for the bidding to start.

The ring was packed with people; standing, sitting and hanging over the rails at the sides. We were too late to get a seat and we had to push to get a decent view.

Lot 1 had been withdrawn so Lot 2 was brought in, a black gelding with a thick neck and short legs, ridden by a girl of about thirteen who looked as if she had been crying.

'The property of Mrs Watts,' the auctioneer announced.

'Preacher, a 10 year old child's pony, excellent gymkhana pony, placed many times. Sadly for sale as owner out-grown,' he continued and the girl wiped a hand across her eyes as she rode Preacher round the ring again as the bidding started. I felt terribly sorry for the girl and swore that I would never sell a pony of mine but would keep him in retirement in lush pastures.

The next horse was an Irish Draught Cross of 18 hands called Sam. 'Quiet in every way,' said the auctioneer, as Sam was neighing loudly to his companions outside, and his words were greeted by laughter, which made Sam neigh even louder. Sam was eventually sold for £1400 and Mari-lyn and I shook our heads in amazement at the thought of so much money changing hands.

The horses and ponies came and went and the afternoon passed very quickly. I had almost forgotten about Heart of Fire when Lot 40 was called for and the beautiful flighty chestnut careered in, almost knocking over his handler. He high-stepped around the ring, shying at the slightest movement and a man with a tweed cap sitting next to us shook his head knowingly.

The bidding started at £200 and went up slowly. Sud-denly a voice beside me said, 'Three-ten' and I looked at Marilyn in astonishment.

'You must be mad!' I hissed. 'We haven't got any money on us.' But her face was determined and I could understand why she wanted the horse, for at that moment I too wanted more than anything to possess Heart of Fire.

'Three-twenty,' said a man's voice at the front.

'Three-thirty,' Marilyn looked grim.

'Three-fifty,' returned the man.

'Three-eighty.'

There was a pause and Marilyn started to relax as the

auctioneer said, 'Going once at three hundred and eighty pounds.'

I hardly recognized my own voice as I shouted, 'Three-ninety!'

Marilyn looked at me with a mixture of bewilderment and disbelief.

'Four hundred,' she said in a quiet voice.

I hesitated. Although Marilyn and I had always shared everything I had known from the moment she saw Heart of Fire that this was one thing she could not share. The minute she had started to bid for Heart of Fire a rift had been created between us which was widened when I bid against her. If she bought Heart of Fire our friendship would never be the same again. If I bought Heart of Fire she would never forgive me. It was too late to go back.

'Four-fifty,' I said decisively.

I will never forget the look of hatred on Marilyn's face as the auctioneer shouted, 'Gone for four hundred and fifty pounds to the lady with the green scarf.'

We sat in icy silence as the last horses were brought in and sold. When it was over I realized with horror that I did not have enough money to pay the 10% deposit. I had two weeks to pay the remainder and Dad would give me a cheque but in the meantime I had to produce £45. I took out my purse and counted. Although I had brought money with me I had spent some of it on the jodhpurs, leaving me with £29.67. My only hope was to borrow the money from Marilyn. I swallowed hard before asking her. She stared at me for a long time and I was certain that she would refuse. If I had been in her shoes I certainly would have done.

'How much did you say you needed? Fifteen pounds?'

'And 33 pence,' I added. 'I'll pay you back with interest.'

111

'All right then. Take it.' She almost flung the money at me.

Heart of Fire was a spirited horse who had been badly schooled, which I learnt as soon as I tried to ride him. I would have to work hard to improve him and I cursed my inexperience. Marilyn would have been able to help but I couldn't bring myself to ask her. After the horse sale I had wondered if we might have a big row but instead we tried to continue as if it had never happened, drifting apart over a period of time. We never mentioned Heart of Fire.

Marilyn spent a lot of time at the riding stables, which made me reluctant to go there and ask for advice. The atmosphere was always strained if we were together and she seemed to lose interest in getting her own horse. Meanwhile Heart of Fire became increasingly difficult to handle, despite my efforts. Many months later, while I was out riding on the moors, I encountered Marilyn sitting under a tree, sketching. She looked up when she heard Heart of Fire and her eyes were full of admiration.

'How are you, Marilyn? I haven't seen you around for a while,' I said casually.

'Oh, I've been staying with friends in Cambridge for the past fortnight. I only got back yesterday,' she replied, her eyes never leaving Heart of Fire.

She got to her feet and started to walk beside me. 'He looks marvellous,' she said, patting his neck.

I nodded and we walked on in silence. The air was turning cold and the wind swept through the trees, bending the branches. It caught one of Marilyn's sketches and suddenly paper was flying everywhere.

'Help me, or I will lose them all,' yelled Marilyn, clutching at the paper with her hands.

'Hang on, then,' I replied, dismounting and running after her.

Before I knew what was happening Marilyn had snatched the reins from my hands and leapt on to Heart of Fire. He reared in surprise and she dug her heels in his side, spurring him into a canter.

'Come back,' I shouted but my words were lost on the wind. My eyes fell on the sketches that had floated to the ground. They were all of a bright chestnut horse with flaxen mane, all Heart of Fire.

I felt helpless as Marilyn and my horse galloped into the distance, her skirt flapping in the wind. A fallen tree loomed before them, blocking their path and they prepared for the take-off. Marilyn did not notice the drop on the landing side and hurtled over Heart of Fire's head as he soared over. She was lying still when I reached her. Heart of Fire was nowhere to be seen.

'This is dull. A hologram of a horsebox.'

Mo had moved on to the next picture but Mark remained behind, all his attention fixed on the open ramp of the horse box.

Horsebox, New Side Panels, Good Condition

' "Horsebox, New side panels, good condition, £300 ono."
Looks just the thing,' announced Linet Alford looking up
from the weekly free newspaper. 'We shall need something
for the show season. I intend to enter Rani for all the major
jumping competitions.'

'I'll arrange to see it tonight, on my way home from
work,' said her father.

'Great. I'll go and tell Rani the good news,' and Linet
rushed off to the stables.

A well-built strawberry roan mare waited in her loose
box, impatient to be fed. She stopped pawing the ground
when she heard Linet's footsteps.

'We've a busy summer ahead, Rani,' said Linet, filling
the haynet. But showjumping was far from Rani's mind as
she grabbed a mouthful of fresh hay, scattering it on the
floor.

'This horsebox is in good condition,' said Mr Alford,
pleased with his buy.

'Good price, too. In fact I beat them down to £250.'

'At least we won't have battles with Rani when she's
loaded into it. She's been in a horsebox dozens of times.
Nice to have our own and not have to borrow all the time.'
Linet commented, brushing her boots. 'The first show is a
week today. I can't wait.'

On the morning of the show Linet was out of bed at the
crack of dawn. Dressed in jeans and T-shirt she fed Rani

and mucked out the stable before focusing her attentions on Rani's appearance. The mare was groomed thoroughly, her tail washed and her mane plaited. Then she was tethered to a ring in the wall to stop her rolling and spoiling Linet's work while her owner grabbed a cup of coffee. With plenty of time to spare, Linet washed and dressed in her best riding clothes and drank more coffee.

'Ready, love?' asked her father.

'Nearly. I'll just load the tack in the horsebox, then I'll get Rani. Mum's making sandwiches for us.'

Rani stepped out jauntily, her head cocked and her tail swishing.

'She looks terrific,' commented Mr Alford. But just as Rani put a forefoot on the ramp she stopped, her ears twitching.

'Come on, silly. You've seen a horsebox before. They're all the same,' laughed Linet. Rani snorted and backed away, evidently nervous.

'Do you want any help?' asked Mr Alford. Linet shook her head irritably. 'I can manage. Come on, Rani.' She pulled on the halter rope but Rani dug her heels in and refused to budge. 'This is ridiculous,' she said in exasperation.

'Let me try.' Her father reached for the halter and Rani stood up on her hindlegs, knocking him back.

Father and daughter spent an hour trying to persuade Rani to enter the horsebox but she steadfastly refused. As time went on, Linet grew more impatient, as she realized in despair that she would be late for her class. Rani was covered in sweat and growing more and more agitated. Even when they blindfolded her before leading her she still would not enter the horsebox.

'This is hopeless,' exclaimed Linet. 'Please, Rani. Please go in.'

Suddenly Rani broke free and galloped out of the yard, jumping the paddock fence and disappearing into the woods.

'What on earth has got into her?' said Mr Alford.

'We'll never catch her, now.'

'Don't worry, Linet, we'll go after her and call the police so they keep an eye out for her.'

But it was not until nearly eleven thirty that night that a neighbour phoned to say that Rani had wandered on to his land and arranged for Linet and her father to collect her the next morning.

'I'll go on foot,' said Linet. 'Somehow I don't think it would be wise to take the horsebox.'

Rani behaved perfectly when she returned home and Linet, although puzzled by her previous behaviour, concluded that the incident must be some kind of fluke abberation; perhaps Rani had been feeling off colour or over excited because of the impending show season. She was bitterly disappointed at having missed the jumping competition but consoled herself with the thought that there were plenty more; in fact, the next big event was in a fortnight.

Linet spent the afternoon schooling Rani and by the evening she had almost forgotten about the incident with the horsebox. However, at supper, her father said, 'I think it would be a good idea to get Rani used to that horsebox. Perhaps we should try again tomorrow.'

'I suppose you're right,' admitted Linet. 'She seems well settled now so I'm sure there won't be a problem.'

Linet took Rani out early to work off any excess energy and minimize any potential problems before confronting her with the horsebox. This time, the minute Rani sighted it in the yard she reared up, her eyes wide with fear.

'Steady, Rani, steady girl, there's nothing to be afraid of,' said Linet, struggling to control her.

'She's really upset,' said Mr Alford. 'If she keeps this up someone will get hurt, most likely herself.' He put the horsebox back in the garage and Rani became calm again.

Linet slept badly that night and awoke feeling hot and thirsty. She threw open the window. The full moon bathed the paddock in silver light and she smiled as she saw Rani grazing in the distance, at the end furthest from the house. Thinking how lucky she was to have such a lovely pony she shuffled downstairs to the kitchen for a glass of milk. As she turned to go back she heard a shrill whinny from outside.

'Quiet, Rani,' she mumbled but the sound continued, growing increasingly louder and Linet began to worry. Convinced that Rani was in pain, she rushed outside, expecting to see her mare standing by the gate, as the whinny sounded very close at hand. But Rani was still grazing in the paddock, too far away for the sound to be hers. Puzzled, Linet tried to locate the sound and slowly realized that it was coming from the direction of the garage.

'My goodness, somehow we've shut a horse in there,' she whispered, racing to unbolt the door. Immediately the sound stopped. She peered into the darkness, wishing she had brought a torch.

'Easy, there, I won't hurt you.' But there was no horse in the garage, only the gardening tools, the jeep and the horsebox.

Suddenly Linet felt overwhelmingly tired and was beginning to wonder if she had imagined it when she heard what sounded like a horse stamping inside the horsebox. Carefully, Linet lowered the door and felt the warm breath of a living being on her face. But the horsebox was empty. A chill travelled down her spine and Linet turned and ran back to the house, leaving the doors open behind her.

At breakfast she apologized to her father, for not shutting the garage door.

'I don't know what you mean, Linet; I've already been out there and all the doors were closed. Had a bad dream?'

'As a matter of fact, yes. A very weird dream,' Linet replied.

As soon as she had finished eating. Linet searched through the old newspapers in the magazine rack to find the one which had advertised the horsebox, praying that it had not been thrown out. She was in luck, and thumbed through the pages until she found the ad, ringed with green biro. She rang the phone number, her heart pounding. A girl who sounded about Linet's age answered.

'Hello, this is Linet Alford; we bought your horsebox last week. The trouble is, my horse won't go near it. Why did you sell it?'

There was an icy silence before the girl replied nervously, 'You'd better talk to my father; it's nothing to do with me,' and the line went quiet. Then a man's voice practically shouted at Linet.

'You got that horsebox for a good price. It's no longer my responsibility,' and the line went dead.

'What on earth is going on?' said Linet aloud.

When her father returned from work Linet confronted him.

'I think we should sell that horsebox.'

'What are you talking about? Don't be ridiculous – we've only just bought it. It was a bargain.' Mr Alford looked irritated.

'There's something odd about it, Dad. Rani knew it from the start. I think the horsebox is haunted.'

Her father laughed. 'Honestly, Linet, the things you come out with. I've never heard such nonsense. Rani is just going to have to get used to it. We'll try her again tomorrow.'

Linet knew that protesting would be hopeless; her father would never believe her.

In the run up to the show, Linet and her father worked hard on Rani and slowly, little by little, the mare would reluctantly walk up the ramp and stand, shivering, in the horsebox. Afterwards, Rani would be in such a state that it took hours before Linet could settle her down again. She grew increasingly apprehensive about the impending show and her anxieties filtered through, not only to Rani, but to her parents. Mr Alford became short-tempered, even threatening to sell Rani if she couldn't learn to behave.

On the morning of the show, Linet awoke with a sick feeling in the pit of her stomach. She dragged herself out of bed and headed for the stable. Rani stood with her head hanging, not at all her usual frisky self. Linet felt that she was going through the motions as she carried out her well-rehearsed routine of feeding, mucking out, grooming and plaiting.

'I couldn't eat a thing, Mum,' she said at breakfast.

'Nonsense, you must eat. You'll feel weak all day if you don't have breakfast,' replied her mother. 'At least have some toast.'

Every mouthful seemed to stick in her throat and Linet was relieved to get back to the stable and Rani.

'Ready, Linet?' asked her father grimly.

'Yes, Dad. Come on, Rani.' Linet led the mare into the yard and faced her at the ramp. Rani sidestepped nervously and stopped with her forefeet on the ramp.

'Go on there,' said Mr Alford sharply, and Rani backed away, knocking him sideways. His face reddened and he reached for a stick.

'No Dad,' pleaded Linet as Rani reared up high, narrowly missing her head on the roof of the horsebox.

Suddenly they heard footsteps on the gravel and a girl's voice yelled, 'Get that horse away from there, quickly!' Linet and her father stood rooted to the spot, amazed at the stranger.

'Get your horse away,' the girl repeated and Linet grabbed Rani's headcollar and pulled her clear of the horsebox.

'What's going on here,' demanded Mr Alford.

The girl looked at Linet. 'You wanted to know why we sold the horsebox? Why it was so cheap?' Linet nodded numbly. 'Because my own pony was killed while being loaded into it. He reared up and hit his head. I can never forget it.' Her face was ashen and her voice trembled.

'How dreadful for you. I'm so sorry,' said Linet, feeling helpless.

'Willow, my pony, he never did like travelling in that horsebox. We had all sorts of problems with him. It used to drive my father mad and he's usually a gentle kind of person. One day, when we were loading him for a show, Willow just went crazy and my father lost his temper and hit him . . .' Her voice went quiet. 'It was awful. Willow hit his head and just fell. Even though it was a year ago, I will never forget. My father will never forgive himself; he blames himself, but it was an accident. Anyway, the horsebox just sat outside, going rusty, and one day Dad said he would do it up and sell it. He gave me the money towards buying another pony.'

'I'm glad you told me,' said Linet gently.

'I had to warn you. Thank goodness I wasn't too late. You have a lovely pony.' Linet and her father exchanged glances and Mr Alford was flooded with guilt. He put his arms around his daughter and hugged her.

'I'll get rid of it, Linet. It will go to the scrapyard.'

The girl turned to go.

'Thank you,' said Linet. 'I do hope you get another pony.' The girl smiled and Linet threw her arms around Rani, trying not to think about what might have been.

The next picture showed a banner which appeared to be flapping in the wind.

The Palio

'Horse number four'. The voice cut through the hushed crowd.

For a minute Angelo felt despair, but the feeling was quickly converted to hope; a flicker that had to be stoked into a flame. This was the first day of the Palio, the oldest horse race in the world. There had to be hope.

The race was the culmination of a year's hard work and sacrifice for Angelo's district, his *contrada*, as his people strove to raise the money needed to pay for the best jockey to ride their allotted horse. The horses had been brought down from the mountain earlier and a random draw selected which horse would represent each *contrada*. The luckiest man in the *contrada* would be sent to receive their horse. Angelo had always been considered lucky. But horse number four was untried so Angelo's people would be disappointed. They had not won a Palio for ten years.

Angelo's mind wandered as he led the horse through the heat haze to the sound of swifts screeching and swooping from the overhead towers. There were fierce rivalries between the *contradas* which surfaced as the Palio approached. The tourists who flocked to Sienna to see the famous race, paying out exorbitant sums to book a seat, only saw the colour and pageantry of the Palio.

'All our hopes rest on you', said Angelo, but the horse, unaware of the responsibility vested in him, simply swished his tail at an irritating fly.

Angelo's family came out to meet them, their faces evidence that they had already heard the news.

'He has never raced. No matter,' said his father. 'We must be hopeful.' He stood back to inspect the horse, who was a deep bloodstone chestnut with a large head. 'He is not pretty. No matter. He is a strong animal. Healthy, too. That is important.' He walked around the horse. 'Good wide chest. Well-sprung ribs. Wide nostrils.'

'He has the markings of a racer, then?' asked Angelo. His father looked thoughtful. 'Perhaps. You must learn to recognize a good animal for when you take over the farm. You should take more of an interest Angelo.' Angelo looked away. He wondered if he would ever be able to tell his father of his real plans and dreams.

Angelo had been chosen to stand guard at the stable until after the race. Anything could happen to the horses, particularly the favourites. Horses had been attacked before by rival *contradas*, so they could take no chances. The bloodstone chestnut paced the loose box, restless and irritable. He scraped at the floor with his foreleg, the noise grating.

'All this fuss over a horse,' muttered Angelo, but he knew that his family and his *contrada* did not see things the same way. The horse continued to pace the stable and his mood infected Angelo. The boy began to feel acutely aware of the enclosed space, of the walls confining them both. For the horse, the confinement would soon be over. But Angelo had felt trapped for years. As the eldest son he was expected to take over the farm when his father retired and from early childhood he had been trained to assume this role. As he grew older and entered his teens he had developed his own interests and started to resist his family.

'This family have always been farmers, since medieval times,' his father said, as if that was a justification. The more his father repeated this, the more Angelo determined not to continue the tradition. But it was not so simple to deny the wishes of his family. Angelo had no wish to hurt them, so he kept bottled his feelings of frustration, loyalty and confusion.

As the hours passed, Angelo began to indentify with the horse. He was relieved when dawn broke and the vet arrived to examine the animal.

'Fit and healthy,' the vet pronounced and as he left, the blacksmith appeared. Angelo's mother came out with food and drink. 'Did you have a quiet night?' she asked her son.

Angelo nodded.

'Why so miserable, son? Is it because of the horse?'

'We should have drawn a different horse, a better horse,' he replied, looking away, reluctant to face her.

His mother shook her head. 'We must be content with what we have. Number four.' She wiped her hands on her apron. 'The horse must have a name.'

'He does. It is Il Trovatore.'

Angelo's mother smiled. 'Yes, The Troubadour – a good name.' In her mind she saw the prize that each *contrada* sought to possess in the race, the ornate flag which bore a picture of the Madonna, patron saint of Sienna. It was this banner which gave the race its name.

'It is a good name,' she repeated. 'It is an omen.'

By midday the heat was oppressive. Angelo needed to get away from the farm but as keeper of the horse he was compelled to stay. When his brother brought him his lunch he saw the opportunity to escape for a while.

'Mario, I have to get away, just for half an hour. Will you take over?'

'It will be an honour.' He frowned. 'But it is breaking the rules. Father would be furious.'

'Then we will not tell him. He is still in the fields.' His eyes pleaded with Mario. 'It is just for half an hour.'

127

'All right,' said Mario, proudly assuming the role of guard.

While Angelo weaved his way through a network of narrow alleyways, the street was being swept free of litter in preparation for the evening trial race. Finally Angelo reached a tiny restaurant, tucked away down a side road on the outskirts of his district. He looked over his shoulder to ensure he was not being followed before slipping inside and sitting at a corner table. He was sipping red wine when the young woman arrived, looking flushed and hot.

'You came,' he whispered. The woman smiled nervously.

'It was not easy to get away.'

'Nor for me. I am supposed to be guarding our horse.'

'The Palio.' Her voice was bitter. 'We drew a good horse. They are hopeful of winning.' She clutched his hand. 'My dear Angelo.'

He smiled. 'Tereza, my dearest sister. How is life?'

'Much as usual,' she replied.

'Do you ever regret marrying into a rival *contrada?* Does your husband's family still treat you as a stranger?'

Tereza sighed. 'It will always be so. The rivalries run deep. They go back many hundreds of years. Old wounds never heal.'

'But how do you bear it?'

'I have to bear it, Angelo. I made a choice when I married. Do mother and father ever speak of me?'

'Never. You committed a terrible crime in their eyes. They will not change.'

'What about you, Angelo. Are you happy?'

His silence answered her question.

'What of the hopes you told me of, of going to art school in London – any news?'

'I sent them a folio of work; drawings, paintings. They have offered me a scholarship.'

Tereza rose from her chair and hugged him. 'Angelo, that is marvellous. What did Father say?'

Angelo looked downcast. 'I cannot tell him. If I went away, it would break his heart. He wants me to run the farm. They would never forgive me.' He kissed her on the forehead. 'I must go, Tereza. I told Mario I would only be half an hour. Father must not find out – '

' – You are afraid. What good is living your life for them if it is like this? Do not live a lie, Angelo.'

As the evening drew on, cannons sounded and each *contrada* brought its horse out for the trial race at the Piazza. Patriotic songs resounded. Despite himself, Angelo felt excited and tense.

Ten horses and riders jostled inside the rope enclosure and the jockeys vied with each other for the best position. Suddenly the horses were off, galloping the first of three circuits on the hard earth of the Piazza. In less than ninety seconds the practice race was over and the horses were being sponged down. The bloodstone chestnut had been blocked at the rope and finished last. Angelo's family could not conceal their disappointment.

The night was cooler than expected and Angelo sat on a straw bale in the corner of the stable watching Il Trovatore. The horse was aloof and kept well away from the boy.

'How can we be sure that our jockey will not betray us?' Angelo's younger sister asked as she sat beside him plaiting straw.

'We can never be completely sure. We have paid our jockey a great deal of money. He has a high reputation.'

'But what if another *contrada* offers him more money to lose?' she persisted.

Angelo shrugged. 'That is the Palio. They are hired outsiders, mostly from Sardinia. We choose them as much for their ruthlessness as for their riding ability. They have to be tough to gallop around the Piazza bareback, risking life and limb. If a jockey loses, he can be beaten up by his contrada for letting them down.'

While Angelo and his sister sat talking, standard bearers – the *alfieri* – practised in the street to the sound of side drummers. Celebration suppers were being prepared for the penultimate evening. Angelo felt acutely aware that all the tensions and struggles of the year were being channelled into a race that lasted only ninety seconds.

The day of the race was heralded by the blessing of the horses by the priest before a respectful crowd. All recited the prayer which culminated in the priest proclaiming, 'Go, and return victorious.'

Banners were tossed high into the air and the costumed processions were greeted by chanting crowds. The horses assembled behind the rope. Their final starting positions had been drawn by lot and revealed only seconds before the race. Angelo looked at his father, who sat behind him, his face drawn and tense. The crowds were grouped together according to their *contrada*, their shouts a mixture of support for their own people and threats directed at rivals. The race had become an emblem for feuding *contradas*. Somewhere in the crowd was Angelo's sister, Tereza, separated from her own family and alienated from her husband's family. Angelo felt suddenly claustrophobic.

'It is important to win, Angelo,' said his father. 'But it is even more important that your enemy loses. Remember this.' Angelo beginning to wonder if it really mattered any more, but he nodded.

'To come second is worse than to come last because you had the chance to win but lost it,' his father continued. 'I would not like to be the jockey who comes in second.'

His words were drowned in the roar of the crowd as the rope dropped and the Palio began.

The favourite was out first, barging into the horse next to him and knocking the jockey off balance. The other horses bumped and jostled as their riders strove to take the lead. Il Trovatore was boxed in for most of the first circuit and Angelo could see from the expression on his father's face that he had given up hope of winning.

By the second circuit of the Piazza the bloodstone chestnut had gained some ground but his jockey seemed engaged in a battle with the jockey who had boxed him in and the two of them were aiming blows at each other with their whips. Suddenly Il Trovatore's jockey was on the ground, leaving his horse to gallop riderless. He challenged the favourite in the final circuit and Angelo's father began to shout encouragement. In the Palio there were no rules and a horse did not require a rider to win the race.

Within seconds the bloodstone chestnut had taken the lead, eating up the ground in long strides. Angelo's *contrada* shrieked its approval and joy as their horse came in first. As the winners hugged each other and the losers swarmed into the Piazza to exact punishment on their jockeys, Angelo could see that Il Trovatore was not going to stop. The big horse did not even check his pace a little but continued to gallop on, through the crowds, out of the Piazza, away from the people. The horse neither knew nor cared that he had brought victory to a *contrada* that had lost for ten years. For him, there was no concept of tradition.

Angelo stared after him, full of admiration and envy. He knew that the horse would not stop until he reached the mountains and freedom.

Mark walked over to the corner.

'This picture has a curious visual effect, depending on what angle you view it from.'

Mo followed his gaze.

'You're right. One minute there appears to be a pony in the far distance; the next it has disappeared.'

Last of the Line

'That looks like the place.'

The smartly dressed man turned to his female companion.

'It must be,' she said. 'Let's hope this is not a wasted journey'.

The cottage nestled at the foot of the valley and could only be approached from the beacon road, which twisted and turned at the sharpest of angles, taking even the most skilled driver by surprise. In the winter, when the snow fell, the road became treacherous and impassable, which suited Ben and his family.

It had been two years since the epidemic and life had settled down to a comparatively normal existence. The village formed a cocoon around the cottage, fiercely protective and sworn to secrecy. Visitors were both feared and discouraged. Conversations were guarded in the presence of strangers, particularly in the pub, where the reporters might lurk.

Curtains parted at the cottage window and a child's face peered out.

'They're here,' she said. 'Come and see, Ben.'

Ben, short and wiry with close-cropped blonde hair edged his young sister out of the way to get a good view.

'Shall I get Mum to let them in?'

Ben nodded. He studied the couple hovering outside by their sleek red Mercedes, sizing them up. His mother went out to greet them, reticent at first, and they followed her inside.

'Mr and Mrs Gaspard, these are my children, Ben and Violet. Say hello, children.'

Violet blushed and Ben shook hands with the Gaspard's in turn, determined to look grown up.

'You look just like your photos,' he said.

'Of course. We're not imposters,' replied Mrs Gaspard, laughing nervously.

'It is an unusual situation. Like you, it is difficult for us to trust people we do not know,' added Mr Gaspard.

'You must be tired after such a long journey,' said Ben's mother. 'Would you like to rest first? We have made a room up for you.'

'Thank you, but we are impatient to see – '

'Follow me,' said Ben, heading outside.

When they reached the stables the visitors gasped.

'The long wait was worth it,' sighed Mrs Gaspard. 'He is truly beautiful.' The object of her adoration was a Highland stallion, mousey dun, his strong black legs feathered with silky hair at the fetlocks and his black dorsal stripe pronounced. He blinked at the visitors through his long forelock.

'This is Buff. I have had him for six years,' said Ben.

'He reminds me of the old days.' Mr Gaspard's voice was wistful.

'I know how lucky I am,' and Ben remembered how afraid he had been when he had first learnt of the mystery virus, brought over from the Continent, that had apparently struck overnight, attacking the nervous system of horses and ponies and killing them within hours. It had swiftly reached epidemic proportions, decimating the horse population, with scientists unable to find a cure. Somehow, miraculously, Buff had remained untouched.

'The last of the line, the last Highland stallion,' said Mr Gaspard. Then he went on to tell of how they had acquired their own horse.

'It was last October, a bitter cold night, wet and miserable. We had travelled up to the Highlands earlier in the day by car, left it on a side road and set off for a walk. It was a remote area and we got lost. We had wandered about for hours and finally sheltered under a clump of trees. Then we noticed a shape huddled beneath them. It was a filly, about eighteen months old, all skin and bone.'

'I bet that was a shock,' commented Violet.

'It was. Horses had already become rare by then. We couldn't believe it,' said Mrs Gaspard. 'She was so tame. Maybe it was because she was weak, I don't know, but she let us lead her home. We made a halter from my scarf.' She groaned. 'It took us hours. We picked the car up the following day.'

'So you adopted her?' asked Ben.

'Yes. We felt blessed. We lavished every care on her and still do. She's quite pretty, a native Highland lass. We called her Lucky.'

'Horses are like gold dust now,' said Ben. 'We've heard that there are only two hundred in the whole of England. They go for incredible prices too, on the black market.'

'I expect you worry about Buff being stolen,' said Mr Gaspard.

'It's always in the back of my mind,' admitted Ben. 'That's why we try and keep Buff a secret. The villagers all help; everyone takes turns to guard him. He's our treasure, our symbol of survival.'

'The city zoo offered us a huge sum for Lucky,' said Mrs Gaspard. 'We would never sell her. We've taken precautions now. We've moved to an island off the Scottish coast, with a group of friends. It's practically a fortress, with sophisticated alarm systems and guard dogs to stop the poachers.'

'It's tragic, this situation,' said Ben's mother. 'Let's hope it won't always be like this.'

Mr Gaspard looked at Ben.

'We have the scope to change things, though. That's what we're here for. When we heard about Buff through a chance acquaintance who had passed through the village and seen you riding we thought it could be the answer to a lot of people's prayers. We did some amateur detective work to track you down.'

'We cannot let the Highland breed die out. If Buff and Lucky were to mate . . .'

'But you live hundreds of miles from here. I would hardly ever get to see Buff if I let you take him. I love my pony. I couldn't bear to be without him.' Ben looked miserable and confused.

The Gaspards rose at six the next morning.

'We need to have a proper talk with Ben,' began Mr Gaspard but Mrs Ellis interrupted.

'Ben's gone. With Buff. He left a note,' she said, her voice tired.

'He doesn't want you to take Buff. He's run off.'

'But where would he go?' asked Mr Gaspard.

'To the moors. That's where he usually goes when he's upset about something. He'll stay away until you've gone. I'm sorry this has been a wasted journey.'

'But we must find him,' said Mrs Gaspard. 'We cannot give up. We'll go after him.'

'I'm afraid he will be difficult to find. Ben knows the moors like the back of his hand.'

The mist was still heavy on the ground when Ben set off.

He had packed a rucksack with enough food for several days and strapped a sleeping bag to the saddle.

This was not the first time Ben had left home. Once, when he and Violet had a violent argument he stayed away on the moors for the whole day. When his father and mother separated and his father moved out of the house and went to live in America, Ben had lived on the moors for two days. It was a peaceful place for him to sort out his thoughts, away from the distractions of people. He breathed in the damp morning air and began to whistle. Buff's ears twitched to the sound. The horse took steady, confident strides and Ben felt secure. He could not bear to be parted from his beloved pony. Throughout the unsettling rows between Ben's parents Buff had remained constant, comfortingly aloof from the problems of human relationships.

Bringing up her children alone, Ben's mother seemed calmer and more relaxed. But Ben loved his father and missed him. It had been two years since he had seen his father and Ben had finally accepted that he may have lost him. He had no intention of losing anything else dear to him. He was determined not to lose Buff.

Pony and boy travelled at a steady pace, only stopping briefly to eat. As the day wore on, the sky darkened. Ben was a little surprised. Rain had not been forecast, but the weather in England could be unpredictable, particularly in the valley. He pulled his hood up.

Within minutes rain was falling, becoming a very heavy torrent, its effect compounded by a sudden high wind. Buff put his head down and walked on unconcerned. Dark clouds began to crowd the sky, blocking out the afternoon light and Ben began to feel unsettled. The ground quickly became waterlogged and Buff's hooves squelched in the sticky mud. Ben wondered if they should seek shelter and turned Buff off the track. He remembered that somewhere there was a ramshackle hut that used to belong to an old hermit and he had an idea that it was a mile off the track. Buff was reluctant to change direction and Ben had to be firm to persuade him to do so. As they progressed, the ground became increasingly soft and Buff slid and stumbled.

'You were right, Buff, we shouldn't have strayed from the path,' said Ben. 'Perhaps we should go back.'

Suddenly Buff squealed and Ben felt mud oozing through his hands. Buff had stumbled into a bog and within seconds he was knee deep in treacherous mud. Ben scrambled to safety on the bank and pulled on the reins to urge Buff to follow. But the horse was stuck solidly and the more he struggled, the deeper he sank. Finally, as if realizing this, Buff stopped moving.

Ben looked around frantically for something he could use to pull the horse out but he was surrounded by mud and grass and nothing else. He could only watch helplessly as Buff was inexorably sucked deeper into the mire. Despair swept over him, both for his own loss and because he realized that if Buff died, the Highland breed died with him.

'Ben!' The unfamiliar voice echoed across the moor and Ben thought he must be imagining things.

'Ben!' The voice repeated. 'Are you there?'

'Over here!' he replied. His relief was tinged with uneasiness as he realized that if they came, they would take Buff away. But if they did not come, Buff would die. 'Quick!' he yelled. 'Buff is dying.'

Mr Gaspard hurried to the sound of Ben's voice, his face tense. Mrs Gaspard was behind him, a thick rope over her shoulder. Her husband made a lassoo and threw it over Buff's head.

'I had a feeling that something bad was going to happen,' Mrs Gaspard said.

'My wife sometimes gets these . . . feelings,' explained Mr Gaspard, hauling on the rope. 'Ben, grab Buff's forelock and pull. We've got to make him move.' Buff was up to his neck in mud, his eyes dull.

'Please try, Buff,' pleaded Ben.

'He's given up,' said Mrs Gaspard.

Suddenly Mr Gaspard pulled his belt off and flicked it at Buff. It stung the pony and he squealed.

'What are you doing?' shrieked Ben, horrified.

But the trick had worked and Buff jumped forward and began to claw at the mud. The two adults and the child pulled on the rope and called encouragement until finally, exhausted, Buff had scrabbled free.

'Let's get you both home,' said Mr Gaspard.

When the boy and pony had been attended to, the Gaspards decided they should leave.

'We've brought enough trouble here. I think it's time we went,' said Mrs Gaspard. 'Thank goodness Ben is safe and Buff is unharmed.'

As they put on their coats and prepared to go, the door opened and Ben came in.

'You should be in bed, child,' said his mother, fussing over him.

'I've been doing some thinking,' he said. 'Out there on the moors, when I thought that Buff would die, I realized how dreadful it would be for the Highland race to die with him. Thankfully, he has survived, but I know that it may only be a matter of time before someone tries to steal Buff and that your security system on the island is more likely to be able to protect the horses than our village watch. If there was a chance for the Highland line to be continued

139

I would be selfish to prevent it, even if it meant losing Buff.'

Mr Gaspard looked at Ben, his face lighting up.

'You mean we can take him?'

Ben nodded, his sombre face breaking into an unexpected smile.

'Besides, Buff might like having a girlfriend!'

'This is interesting. Two ponies and traps engaged in a race,' said Mark. 'It all looks old-fashioned – like in those television period dramas. Like Northanger Abbey or Vanity Fair. I wonder what they are racing for.'

Mo felt excited.

'It's as if the race has been frozen in time; as if some invisible force is holding them back. I wish we could release them.'

Regency Dandy

'Sophie, dear, we leave for Brighton tomorrow. We will stay with cousin Charlotte. I do so love the season.'

Sophie smiled uncertainly at her mother who bustled, excited at the prospect of escaping from what was for her the dull routine of country life in 1812.

'But what about Catkin? Who will take care of him?'

'What a fuss over a silly pony. Your father and brother will ensure he wants for nothing.'

'I will miss him terribly,' Sophie looked downcast and her mother took her gently by the hands and knelt beside her.

'Sophie, you are sixteen years of age: you are a lady and must learn to behave as befits a lady. Ponies and dogs are all very well for children, but this is your first season. You should be excited at the prospect of your introduction to the real world.' She cast a critical eye over her young daughter. 'We must acquire a new wardrobe for you, child. White muslin may be suitable for the country but . . .'

But Sophie had stopped listening and in her mind she was galloping across the hills on her white pony, Catkin. He was a stocky animal, with short legs and a slightly large head but to Sophie he was the prettiest pony in the world. What he lacked in breeding he made up for in courage, being a game pony and bold over the jumps. Catkin had been with Sophie for as long as she could remember – a gift from her father when she was still a toddler, despite disapproving noises from her mother. Catkin had been past his prime even then and no one was certain how old he was now. Although the pony still acted like a youngster Sophie knew that soon she would have to retire him.

'. . . and a velvet gown, trimmed with swansdown is considered to be the very height of fashion . . .' Her mother's voice seemed to drift in and out of her ears like a passing breeze and Sophie was compelled to think about their impending excursion.

The season lasted from April to July and consisted of garden parties, balls, theatre visits and a great number of shopping trips. The rest of the time would be spent paying and receiving social calls and exchanging gossip.

'This visit to Brighton is going to be very tiresome,' commented Sophie as she stared through the open window at Catkin grazing outside.

'Nonsense. Brighton is the most fashionable and exciting place. It was merely a fishing village when the Prince Regent first visited, but he has transformed it. We can visit the Pavilion, that most renowned of palaces.'

'Will there be ponies?'

Sophie's mother frowned. 'No. I don't want to hear ponies or horses mentioned again, either before or during our visit. Now, go and get ready for dinner.'

The journey to Brighton by coach was long and tedious. The roads were dirty, the uneven surfaces treacherous for the horses and also for the passengers. Most travellers went by foot and the roads were busy with farmers driving their herds of cattle, sheep or geese, as well as packhorses carrying coal, fish or lime.

They shared the coach with another mother and daughter who were also journeying to Brighton for the season, and though she was encouraged to make polite conversation Sophie could think of nothing to say. She was relieved when they reached Brighton and she was able to escape from the ladies' incessant chatter about hats or foreign influence on furniture styles.

Feeling tired and aching after the bone-jarring coach journey, she stifled a yawn when she was introduced to cousin Charlotte.

She stared around the room, tastefully decorated in lavender buff, with chintz draperies and flower-stands of basket work in every corner. Cousin Charlotte herself looked the epitome of good taste, dressed in white satin trimmed with rolls and frills. She regarded her country cousin with a faintly superior air.

'I took the liberty of purchasing for Sophie an evening gown. It is laid out on your bed, dear.' She leaned across to Sophie's mother in a confidential manner. 'It is cut very square and low over the bosom. Most becoming for a young woman.' Then, to Sophie, 'Do try it on; we shall be impatient to see it.'

Later that evening, when Sophie was finally allowed to retire to bed, she lay awake for hours, thankful to be rid of the uncomfortable dress and wishing she was back at home. She had bade a tearful farewell to Catkin and her brother had promised faithfully to take care of him for her. If only she had been born a boy. She could stay at home and ride and climb trees, without having to pay court to nonsense about fashion and polite society.

The next morning, however, a surprise visitor encouraged her to hope that perhaps the stay in Brighton would not be nearly as dull as she had thought.

'This is George Billings, our next door neighbour. His mother is a dear friend,' said cousin Charlotte.

George Billings smiled across at Sophie, his brown eyes kind, his face animated.

'I wondered if perhaps you would care to ride with me

in my carriage. With your mother accompanying us, of course,' he added hastily.

'We would be delighted, wouldn't we, Sophie,' replied her mother.

Sophie stopped to make friends with George's chestnut pony before getting into the carriage.

'Do you like her?' asked George. 'She is called Dawn.'

'She is charming,' replied Sophie.

'Sophie is somewhat obsessive about horses,' explained her mother.

They spent a pleasant hour riding with George, who was both an excellent driver and a good conversationalist. Sophie was delighted when George invited her to go on a picnic on the beach the following day, weather permitting.

So, contrary to her expectations, Sophie found herself enjoying her first week in Brighton. The town seemed more interesting with George for company and even the interminable dinner parties and shopping trips became bearable.

One morning, while she was reading a letter from her brother assuring her that Catkin was as fit and lively as ever, she noticed a stranger standing in the doorway of the parlour.

'You must be Sophie,' he said, his dark eyes holding her transfixed. 'I am Charlotte's brother, your cousin Edmund.'

Distant memories of her childhood flickered; of games of hide and seek with an arrogant youth who hated to lose, of being teased and having her hair pulled. She looked up at the young man.

'You have grown, cousin,' said Edmund.

'You also,' she replied, getting to her feet. It was hard to equate this tall gentlemen, dressed in the military fashion with gold braid and epaulettes, with her cousin Edmund.

146

'Perhaps you would do me the honour of accompanying me on the promenade?' he said, offering her his arm.

Sophie was fascinated by Edmund's tales of adventure and travel abroad and briefly forgot that George was to visit her that afternoon. She arrived back late, to George's irritation. She felt reluctant to part from Edmund and George's conversation seemed suddenly dull by comparison. But George was not to be outdone and an invitation to a new play soon restored Sophie's interest.

As the season progressed Edmund and George began to vie for Sophie's attention, which she found both flattering and amusing. Edmund, having more income at his disposal, found it easier to impress Sophie, constantly buying her gifts. He was an enthusiastic follower of fashion and was always attired in the latest clothes.

'He is nothing but a fopling, a dandy,' said George scornfully. 'Really, Sophie, I don't know what you see in the man.'

'You are jealous, George. Besides, Edmund is getting a new horse for his gig. He is taking me out in it tomorrow morning.'

'But you promised to ride with me tomorrow morning,' George protested.

'I'm sorry, George, I admit that I had forgotten. I should love to see the new horse though.'

'Women are so fickle,' said George wearily. 'However, I shall not hold you to your promise.'

'Thank you, George.' Sophie kissed him lightly on the forehead.

'But I shall expect to take you to the ball tomorrow night.' Sophie smiled, but said nothing.

Edmund's new horse was a handsome bay with clean limbs and a proud head, if a little lightweight.

'What is he called?' asked Sophie.

'He is not named, as yet. You shall decide.'

When Sophie put out her hand to the horse he threw up his head nervously, backing into the stable. 'Oh,' said Sophie in surprise. 'He seems a little jumpy.'

'He is young and green,' said Edmund. 'He will have to learn.' There was a tone in his voice that made her feel uncomfortable, a tone she had never noticed before.

The horse still looked unsettled in harness and Sophie felt anxious.

'He looks showy, does he not?' said Edmund proudly. 'I am assured he is very fast.'

The horse went forward abruptly in a rather unbalanced manner. His paces were not at all smooth and Sophie did not enjoy the ride.

When they arrived back George was waiting on the front steps by his pony and gig.

'I hope you had a pleasant ride,' he said stiffly, helping Sophie out.

'Edmund's new horse is a showy beast, too showy – no substance. Like his owner,' he said, raising his voice. 'A fop.' Turning to Sophie he said, 'I will collect you at seven for the ball.'

'Pardon me, sir, but the lady will be accompanying me to the ball,' said Edmund.

'Is this true, Sophie?' George demanded.

Sophie blushed. 'I have not decided yet. I do not wish to offend either of you.'

'Then we shall decide,' said Edmund. 'We shall fight for your hand.' He turned to George. 'You think yourself an expert horseman. I challenge you to a race – horse and gig. The winner claims Sophie. What do you say, sir?'

Sophie looked aghast. 'I am not a prize to be won. I will not allow such folly.'

'I accept your challenge, Edmund,' said George, ignoring her protests.

'When will the race commence?'

'Now.'

'Immediately?'

'Having second thoughts? Your horse is ready, is she not?'

'Now, then.' George sprang into his gig.

'To the beacon and back,' yelled Edmund, cracking his whip and before Sophie knew it they had disappeared in a cloud of dust. Panicking, she rushed into the house, shouting, 'Help me, we must stop them or they will surely kill each other.'

The dust stung his eyes as George urged his horse faster. His chestnut mare, Dawn, was a good horse and he had no wish to ruin her, but the thrill of the chase had overtaken his common sense. Dawn stretched her neck eagerly as George made encouraging noises above the sound of the wheels. Edmund was well ahead, the unnamed bay horse a swifter animal than Dawn.

Edmund crouched forward on the edge of his seat, arms outstretched, the reins in his left hand and the whip in his right, ready to remind his horse who was in charge. Edmund was not prepared to lose, and he was already picturing the look of envy on his rival's face when he, Edmund, was Sophie's partner at the ball.

When his horse stumbled he swore, lashing with the whip. The horse galloped forward, his shoulders stinging from the cut of the whip. His previous owner had been an impatient man, showing no kindness when breaking him to harness and the horse remembered this clearly, regarding both men and carriages with fear. He associated any disobedience with punishment and despite his feet being cut and made sore by the sharp stones he continued to race ahead.

As they rounded the bend and approached the home straight, George unexpectedly drew level with Edmund, who lashed at his rival with the whip, catching George's face with the lash. The race had become deadly serious. Taken aback, George lost speed and Edmund pulled away as the road curved downhill.

The terrain was rugged and dangerous but Edmund did not seem to notice and, intoxicated by speed and his impending victory, he continued to hit the unfortunate bay horse, who was beginning to tire. Suddenly the wheel hit a boulder and the gig overturned, spokes and axle splintering, and the bay horse fell on its side.

Sophie had persuaded a groom to pursue the racers and they drew up in a dog-cart, just in time to witness the accident. George, who had caught up by now, rushed to the horse who was lying very still.

'Is he dead?' Sophie was trembling.

'What about me?' demanded Edmund getting to his feet, blood trickling from a wound to his head.

'No more than concussion,' grunted the groom. 'Think yourself fortunate.' He knelt by the horse. 'We have to get him up.'

After a good deal of encouragement the horse was persuaded to stand. He was shivering and the groom laid his coat across the animal.

'He's covered in weals,' gasped Sophie, revolted at the sight.

'Edmund has a sadistic streak,' commented George. 'I should have told you, but I knew you would not believe me. You seemed besotted with Edmund.'

Sophie looked sheepish. 'All that matters now is getting this horse well.'

Remarkably, the horse had not broken any bones but a bruise to his near foreleg had made him lame and he limped painfully.

'Poor lamb,' whispered Sophie. 'You should be ashamed of yourself,' she said to Edmund.

'I suppose this means you won't be coming with me to the ball tonight?' Edmund said.

'Are you mad? I never want to see you again.' Sophie's face was red with rage.

'Since you care more about horses than men you can keep that broken-down nag. I have no more use for it. I will be leaving for London this evening. Goodbye, cousin.'

When he had gone George said, 'What will you do with this poor unfortunate horse? It would certainly be foolish to try and put him in harness for a very long time, if ever. After such an experience the poor beast may be good for nothing.'

Sophie looked sad. 'You are probably right, George. It is tragic to think that if things had been different, if he had been blessed with a caring owner – ' She broke off. 'Perhaps there is hope after all. Edmund gave the horse to me. I could care for him properly in the country. He may yet make a good riding horse.' She smiled. 'He would make a companion for my dear Catkin.'

'I am sorry this happened. I should never have raced Edmund,' said George.

Sophie was silent for a while. Then she said, 'Edmund wished for me to name the horse.'

'The horse is yours now.'

'Despite his behaviour, I shall find it hard to forget Edmund.'

'He was fond of you, Sophie. As I am,' said George. The horse stumbled, knocking Sophie off balance and the groom insisted that she ride in the dog-cart.

151

As soon as they arrived back the groom assumed responsibility for the horse, promising Sophie that he would use all of his skills to repair the injuries. George hovered in the doorway before taking his leave.

'Goodbye, Sophie. I hope that your horse recovers.'

'Goodbye, George. There will be other balls. The season is not over yet. I have a name for my horse. He will be my Dandy.'

As they walked over to the next picture, Mo said, 'I'm sure I can smell burning.' They looked round but could see no source of the smell. 'It's coming from over here. It's coming from this picture!' said Mo.

No Ill Effects

The smell of burning straw attacked her nostrils and Claire panicked. Through the smoke she could make out the shape of a horse kicking, terrified, at the strong wooden door. Claire wrenched and pulled at the door, splinters tearing at her skin and burying themselves under her nails.

The flames were all around, overpowering her, the fumes seeping into her throat and lungs. All her strength was draining away; she could not even shout for someone to help her rescue the trapped horse. Suddenly she was coughing, fighting for breath as if a heavy weight was pressing on her chest . . .

'Claire! Wake up! You're having a nightmare!' Her mother was beside her, warm and reassuring. 'It's all right, Claire. You're safe.'

Claire shivered. 'It was the same dream again. Every night since we've been living here.'

'I'll get you a drink, dear.'

By the time she had returned from the kitchen, her daughter had drifted back into an uneasy sleep.

The next morning, Claire woke feeling irritable and tired, her head pounding.

'You've had the same dream for a week now,' said her mother, over breakfast. 'Perhaps we should call the doctor.'

Claire shrugged. 'What could he do?'

'I expect it's sleeping in a strange house,' suggested her father. 'It takes some getting used to. You do like it here, don't you?'

Claire gazed into her coffee cup, thinking about the friends she would miss and the new ones she would have to make at the new school.

Since her father's promotion they had all agreed that it would be sensible to move in to the town, so he could be nearer to the office. Claire could not object to living in a bigger house, which they were now able to afford, and one which had a stable and paddock. No more cycling five miles in rain or shine to the rented field where she had kept Kahlia, her Arab mare.

She had owned Kahlia for a year now, and the horse was her pride and joy, with her copper chestnut coat as soft as a kid glove. Her dish face had all the unmistakeable characteristics of the Arabian horse, with dark eyes and bell-shaped nostrils.

'It's a lovely house,' Claire said. 'Now I think I'll take Kahlia out for some exercise.'

Claire had intended to explore her new surroundings at the first opportunity, but the house was still full of boxes and packing cases, so instead she had spent most of her time helping her mother.

Kahlia seemed pleased to see her and Claire was feeling more animated by the time she had groomed and tacked up the mare. Kahlia was frisky and full of beans. She did not like being stabled for too long but the paddock was currently waterlogged so there was no alternative.

'Hang on, there,' cried Claire, hopping along with one foot in the stirrup as Kahlia decided to move off while her rider was trying to mount.

The mare strode out keenly and Claire could feel the energy coiled beneath her like a tightened spring. Kahlia took an interest in her new surroundings, peering over garden gates and pricking her ears at the slightest sound.

Claire started to whistle and wondered if there were any more people in the neighbourhood who rode.

When they rounded the corner Claire did not notice the roadworks sign and the hole in the road flanked by flashing yellow lights, but Kahlia saw it immediately. Her legs stiffened and she stood completely still, her eyes nearly popping out at the sight that met her.

'Don't be silly, Kahlia. It won't hurt you.' Claire nudged the mare with her heels.

Kahlia started to run backwards, slipping on the wet tarmac in her panic.

'Stop it, Kahlia! I'm not in the mood for this,' Claire snapped.

Ten minutes soon passed, with neither horse nor rider prepared to give in, when an unfamiliar voice said, 'Do you need any help?' A wiry boy with close cropped blond hair and tattoos on his arms was standing behind her.

'Thanks. Could you just get hold of the bridle and lead her past that hole?'

'Sounds simple enough,' said the boy.

'But be careful. Kahlia can be a bit wary of strangers.'

The boy was self-assured and his command of the situation seemed to impress Kahlia, who walked calmly past the obstacle that minutes before had terrified her.

'Nice looking horse,' commented the boy.

'Do you ride?' asked Claire.

The boy laughed. 'You're joking. I don't know the first thing about horses.'

He continued holding the reins. 'You must be Claire.'

'How did you know?' Claire began to feel nervous.

'Saw you move in last week. I live two doors away.' He smiled. 'I'm Andy, by the way.'

'You certainly are,' replied Claire, and they both laughed at the joke.

157

'See you around, then,' he said, turning off at the end of the road.

The smoke had become so thick it was impossible to breathe. Claire covered her face with a scarf, but she was still coughing and spluttering. Inches away she made out the outline of the horse, tethered to a ring in the wall and unable to escape. She reached out and the mare reared up, the whites of her eyes showing. 'Kahlia!'

Claire awoke drenched in sweat, her breathing rapid and shallow. Her mother rushed in.

'It was that terrible dream again. This time I saw the horse. It was Kahlia,' said Claire.

The next day, while Claire was mucking out the stable, Andy paid a visit.

'You look a bit rough this morning. Are you not feeling well?' he asked.

'I didn't sleep well,' she replied. 'I had a bad dream.' She leaned the pitchfork against the door and looked at him. 'I keep having it, every night since we moved in.'

'Tell me about it.'

When Claire had related her dream he said, 'I used to have a recurring dream, when I was five. I remember it clearly. I am lying in bed when an old lady comes in and walks towards me. I don't know who she is, but she comes over and looks as if she is going to say something. Then she changes her mind, turns round and walks away.' He stared glassy-eyed at her. 'I've never told anyone about that dream.'

'Was it scary?' asked Claire. He shook his head. 'No. Just . . . sort of disturbing. Anyway, it stopped after a few years.'

'A few years! I hope my dream doesn't go on for that long.'

That night Claire decided to go up to bed early and read. She felt tense, dreading sleep in case the dream recurred. As she went up the stairs her mother said, 'I hope you don't get too friendly with that boy who was here today.'

'Why ever not? He's really nice.'

'I've heard things about him from the lady next door.'

'You mean gossip,' laughed Claire.

'She says he's on probation.'

'As long as it's not for arson,' said Claire, laughing nervously.

The wood fractured with a sickening crash and exploded into flames, setting the straw alight. The horse squealed and then all that could be heard was the crackling of the flames . . .

Claire screamed. 'The stable's on fire. Kahlia!' She hurtled down the stairs and fumbled with the lock, leaving the burglar alarm to whine when the door flew open. She ran outside, her bare feet squelching in the mud. Her parents, awakened by the noise, followed close behind.

'What the devil is going on?' Her father looked worried and angry.

'The stable – I thought it was on fire.'

'Well, you can see it isn't, so for goodness' sake let's get back inside.'

Her mother took Claire's hand, seeing what had happened. 'Maybe you should see a doctor.'

'Can't we put Kahlia in the paddock tonight? She's not safe in the stable,' said Claire.

'Don't be silly. Nothing is going to happen. Anyway, you know the field is too wet. But if it makes you feel better, I'm sure your father will check the stable to be certain.'

By the morning, the weather had improved and Claire's mother suggested that she went for a ride to unwind.

'There's a park a mile away where you can take horses. I've heard that local riders use it quite a bit. You might meet some new people.'

'Other than Andy, you mean,' said Claire. 'But you're right about the park, Kahlia could do with a good gallop.'

Kahlia practically skipped along the road, shying at every opportunity and Claire was relieved to let the reins out so the mare could let off steam. They were slowing to a canter when a horse and rider suddenly shot out from behind a hedge straight in front of them. Startled, Kahlia slid to a halt and Claire shot off over her head.

'I'm so sorry,' said the other rider, a girl about Claire's age. 'I'm afraid Rab bolted – ' She stopped short and stared at Kahlia.

'Why, it's Kahlia, isn't it? I'd recognize that horse anywhere!'

Claire got to her feet, rubbing her grass-stained jodhpurs. 'You know her? How?'

'I should do – I used to own her.' The girl smiled uncertainly. 'How do you find her then? To ride and that.'

'She's perfect,' replied Claire.

'Thank goodness. I felt a bit guilty really, putting her in the sale so quickly. No ill effects, then?'

'Ill effects?' Claire looked puzzled.

'There was an accident, just before we sold her. But she's obviously got over it.'

'What accident?'

'Luckily she was rescued in time. But for a while she got trapped when the stable caught fire.'

160

'*A landscape, beautiful but bleak. Imagine living out there.*'
'*We don't have to imagine.*'

Brumby

Sal stared across the barren landscape. It was the dry season, when many of the inland rivers were no more than a series of waterholes. Beyond the grasslands stretched the desert, a huge dust heap, vast and monotonous. The red earth seemed to shimmer under the merciless white sun. Sal had ambivalent feelings for the country. She loved the vastness of the land, the starkness of the landscape evoking primeval beauty, but she hated it for the hardship it imposed on the people, making their difficult lives nearly impossible.

One hundred years had passed since Captain Cook first set foot on Australian soil in 1770, followed by the English convicts who were the enforced pioneers, Sal's ancestors.

Conditions were still tough and Sal's family eked out a meagre living on their small farm, growing wheat and raising sheep. The climate and the distance were their worst enemies. The nearest town was three days walking, and Sal's youngest brother had died because it had taken too long to fetch the doctor before pneumonia had claimed him. Since that tragedy the family had acquired a horse, a scrubby mare called Peg. She was already long in the tooth but she had been cheap and had enough years left as a working animal to make the transaction worthwhile.

When times were particularly tough and money in even shorter supply than usual, her father would go out on the road to find extra income, working as a drover or shearer or handyman, often going for months at a time, leaving her mother to cope with the home and four children.

Sal felt relieved when her father was away, fearing his drunken rages, when he took out his frustration on his family. Her parents were always shouting and arguing. Sal had determined never to marry.

A gathering dust cloud in the distance, choking and blinding her as it came nearer, brought Sal abruptly back to the present and excitement boiled up inside her as the herd of brumbies approached. These brumbies were descendents of the domestic horses turned loose on the ranges during the gold-rush, 'brumby' being adapted from the aboriginal word for wild.

They had been here, to this diminishing waterhole, every day this week, at about the same time, early evening. As usual, the stallion led, checking out the place for unwelcome visitors. Finally, when he was sure it was safe, he stood back to let the smallest and weakest of the herd drink first, keeping watch. Only when they had drunk their fill would he drink.

Sal stayed hidden behind a boulder, downwind of the cautious stallion. He was a handsome animal, dark bay, with a jagged white blaze. Like all the horses, his coat was scrubby and dusty and his ribs showed. The dry season would claim the weakest of the herd, Sal thought, with regret.

But it was not the stallion that her attention was focused on. One of his sons, a colt, had caught her eye when she first saw the herd a week ago, awakening a deep desire to tame and possess him. He was a blue roan, his coat marbled grey and blue, his mane and tail a darker iron grey. His nostrils flared, his ears twitched back and forth continually; like his father, he listened for the slightest sound, at which the herd would retreat, disappearing in a flash, leaving only their prints in the dust to testify of their existence.

The stallion was already well marked with war wounds, scratches and scars decorating his muscular neck and flanks. The colt would one day assume his father's role, defeating the stallion in battle or driving him away to die. Sal was filled with admiration for the blue colt. But what fascinated her most about him was his unusual eyes; they marked him out from any horse she had ever seen, making him special, supernatural even. The colt turned to look up at the boulders and she saw clearly that one eye was blue, like his coat, and the other a golden amber.

That night, as Sal lay in bed in the little shack that was her home, she thought about the blue horse and wondered how she might catch him. The waterhole was drying up and the herd would very soon move on to find more precious water, travelling long distances, so that she might never see them again.

When she was feeding the hens the next morning she asked her older brother Davey for advice.

'You won't catch no brumby,' he said scornfully. 'Men've tried and failed. If a man can't do it then a girl damn well couldn't!'

'Why not?' she demanded, but Davey just laughed and continued to chop wood.

'If you're so clever how would you do it?' she persisted.

'I wouldn't,' said Davey. 'Brumbies are vermin. Should be shot. That stallion stole all Henry Clark's mares the other month. They could ruin a man.' He wiped his arm across his brow. 'Better keep an eye on old Peg, I reckon.'

But Sal refused to listen, determined that she could achieve what others had failed to do. It occupied her mind while she did the daily chores and claimed her dreams until she was obsessed by the wild brumby.

She set out in the dawn, loud with the shrieks of green parrots, a rope slung over her shoulder. She passed pink rocks and bleached bones, testaments to the past, and watched a sluggish goanna take up a statuesque pose at her approach.

She waited patiently at the waterhole for what seemed like hours. The sun scorched the red earth and Sal pulled her hat forwards to protect her face from peeling. She was just beginning to wonder if she was too late, that the brumbies had already moved to another waterhole, when she heard their hooves in the dust. She watched the stallion lead as usual, watched the herd descend, mares and foals first, to drink their fill.

Her eye picked out the blue colt in the middle of a bunch and she knew that if he stayed in that position she would have no chance of roping him. But there was jostling among the colts, a squabble about the roan's position in the hierarchy and after some nipping the blue moved nearer to the front, standing a little to the side.

Sal saw her chance and, standing up in an instant, threw the rope. It whistled through the air but the stallion had given warning before it had left her hand, and the herd were disappearing. Her heart sank, knowing that the herd would not return to this waterhole, remembering the danger. Then through the dust she saw, disbelieving, the blue roan on his side in the shallow, muddy water. She hesitated.

In the panic the roan had slipped and fallen and been kicked by another colt taking flight. He had been stunned temporarily, but now he was recovering and clambering to his feet. The whole event had only taken seconds but Sal felt she was seeing it all in slow motion as she pulled her rope in and threw again. Still tottering, the horse did not

166

have time to elude the rope and it landed neatly over his head. Quickly, Sal wrapped the rope round the rock.

The brumby threw up his head, pulling the rope tighter, and shrieked his indignation. He reared up, his sharp hooves clawing the air and his nostrils flared in fury. For the first time Sal felt afraid and the realization of what she had done hit her with force. The horse was wild and dangerous. If she tried to get near him she would probably be kicked.

For the next few minutes Sal just sat on the rock and stared, unsure of what to do next. She had to summon all her courage to face the furious animal. The brumby eyed her suspiciously despite her encouraging murmurings, her soothing words. They were both trembling.

He was a beautiful horse, growing more beautiful as she inched closer and closer to the flashing hooves. In her mind she was taming him, winning him over with her love, gaining his trust. She was riding the blue brumby, galloping bareback across the outback, away from her harsh life, alone with her horse.

Suddenly the picture changed and she saw instead a tired horse, with saddle sores and a dusty coat, his spirit broken, like Peg. The life of a farm horse was all hard work and little play, like her own. Her father would never allow her to keep the horse without ruining it and the horse would be defeated or die. How could she inflict such a fate on the brumby?

She extended her hand to the brumby in a gesture of friendship. Tentatively, he breathed into her palm. Time stood still for the horse and the girl and for a brief moment the dream became reality. Then the brumby jerked back, pulling on the rope. She took a knife from her pocket and swiftly cut the rope.

The colt swung round on his heels and galloped, disappearing in a cloud of dust.

Life went on as usual for Sal and her family. The only change to the routine occurred nearly a year later when Peg, despite her years, gave birth to a foal, a honey-brown colt. It was only Sal that did not comment on the foal's unusual eyes – one a piercing blue, the other a warm amber.

'Hey, there's a slide-viewer on this table,' Mark picked it up and looked into it.

Extras

Exterior. 1890. Transylvania. Night. A track in the middle of a forest.

Horses' hooves are heard rapidly approaching. A hearse pulled by two black horses comes into view and thunders past. Silence, then a coach pulled by two white horses is seen galloping furiously in pursuit. Quick pan following the coach reveals the rest of the track sloping up to a distant castle. A flash of lightning.

'Cut! And get those horses off the set. We haven't got all night!'

'What's the matter with him today?'

'He probably got out of bed the wrong side.'

'I thought that scene went particularly well. I always enjoy vampire films. Great fun.'

'But don't you find you always get typecast, being black?'

'Well I suppose so, but it's a crust, isn't it? Work is thin on the ground these days. You're with an agency, aren't you? They're very commercially orientated. I'm with a trainer. He's well-known in the industry.'

'I know. You were in Black Beauty, weren't you?'

'Yes. I was one of the six horses who played the lead.'

'Made a change to play the hero, I expect. It gets so boring always playing the villain's horse. Still, it beats working at a riding school.'

'Done that, have you?'

'In my youth. Being pushed around by a load of kids who haven't a clue how to treat a horse. Kicking your ribs and pulling at your mouth. It's a crying shame that a noble animal such as myself has to sink to such depths. In fact, I am always being complimented on my appearance. It's the distinctive white half-moon on my forehead that marks me out from the rest. Of course, they have blacked it out for this film.'

'Oh well, it looks as if they're ready to shoot the next scene. Here we go again.'

Exterior. The castle grounds. Night. An open grave.
The hearse arrives. Tracking shot following the Count as he jumps out of the hearse followed by the girl. They are making for two coffins in the grave. The Vampire Hunter and Franz are lying in wait for them. The count sees them and escapes, but by now the girl has climbed into her coffin. They seize her and hold her down. The Vampire Hunter produces a sharpened stake.
VAMPIRE HUNTER
I mean to drive this through her heart.
FRANZ
For pity's sake –
VAMPIRE HUNTER
You must understand, Franz. What you see before you is no longer your daughter. She is but a vessel for the Count's evil!
FRANZ
I cannot bring myself to watch.
VAMPIRE HUNTER
As you hope for your salvation and that of your daughter, you must assist me. Hold the torch near.
He drives the stake through her heart. She lets out a bloodcurdling scream.

'That's it for the evening. I could do with some supper.'
'Too right. I could murder a bucket of oats.'

172

'You'll be lucky. I bet we just get boring old hay again.'

'Low standard of cuisine here. This morning's hay was musty. Not very impressive. Now if we were the stars and not just the extras . . .'

'Jobs are so sporadic at the moment. Not many westerns around. It's all police chases and science fiction.'

'I've had some interesting jobs recently. One or two commercials and a historical costume drama for the BBC, pulling a coach.'

'You're lucky then. My agent isn't too hot at the moment. If you ask me, he drinks too much.'

'Rumour has it that he's a compulsive gambler too. Apparently he's having trouble paying his debts.'

'Well, our part in the film is nearly finished. It should be all over tomorrow, bar the shouting.'

'Then on to the next job.'

'If there is a next job.'

The forest outside the castle. Moonlit night.
Long shot of the hearse thundering down the track, driven by the Count. The girl is leaning out, screaming.

'Thank goodness that's over. That actor could do with some lessons in driving a coach. I could have broken my legs galloping down the hill at that speed.'

'Still, it's a job, isn't it? Better than a poke in the eye with a sharp stick.'

'Oh, so you've been in Equus too.'

'Very funny. I hope someone soon takes this ridiculous plume off my head.'

'I wonder what we'll be doing next. A rest wouldn't come amiss.'

'I overheard my trainer talking to one of the grooms. It looks as if I'm on the shortlist for the leading role in the remake of *National Velvet*. I don't know how to tell you this, mate, but I also heard him say that your agent has gone bust. He'll have to sell everything he owns.'

'Including me. Who's going to want a redundant film horse?'

'It's a great pity. You're still in your prime. Don't worry. Something will turn up.'

'You mean, like in the movies – '

'Closing time!'

Mark and Mo turned to see the gallery attendant standing behind them, tapping his foot impatiently.

'The gallery is closed,' The man pointed to his watch.

'I think he's trying to tell us something,' said Mark.

'But I wanted to find out what happened to the film horse . . .'

'Come on, Mo, we'd better go.'

When they got outside, the children were surprised to discover that it was starting to get dark.

'We must have spent the whole day in the gallery. But the time went so quickly,' said Mark.

The bus journey home was slow and tedious, the driver having to compete with the rush hour traffic.

Their stop was on the housing estate, on the edge of town. They walked in silence, the street lamps shedding an eerie light across the path.

As they neared their house Mo said, 'We didn't imagine it, did we? I mean, you saw it too.'

'It was more experiencing something than just seeing it. Maybe we were sharing some kind of telepathic experience; twins sometimes do. I've read about that kind of thing,' replied Mark.

Mo laughed. 'Listen to us! Talk about imagination! It's obvious, isn't it? It was all part of the exhibition – like those museums where the exhibits move and talk and teach you things.'

174

Mark nodded. 'You're probably right.'

The front door opened.

'You're late,' said their mother. 'Your father has been home from work for an hour. We were waiting for you.'

'I nearly forgot – it's our birthday,' laughed Mo, noticing the birthday cake on the kitchen table.

'Did you have a good day?' asked their father.

'Oh yes,' replied Mark. 'Much better than we expected.'

'Well, before we sit down, you'd better have your birthday present.' Their mother ushered them into the garden. Standing before them was a black horse.

'I hope you like him.' Their mother was grinning.

'He's great,' said Mark and the horse began to walk towards them, hoping for titbits.

'Don't you think he's handsome?' asked their mother. 'His face looks so attractive with that lovely little half-moon shape on his forehead.'

Mark and Mo exchanged a knowing look and Mo said, 'Oh yes, he's a star all right.'